This books is dedicated to all those who have suffered silently with their mental health. Art can help you heal.

PURGATORY; ARCHAIC

A collection of short plays and monologues for actors.

CONTENTS

Plays

Monologues

CONFESSION

Confession was first performed at The International Bar, Dublin on November 15th, 2017. The cast was as follows:
Father Donnelly Barry McBrien
Heather Jones Joan Fleetwood
Director Luke Corcoran
Produced by The Collective productions

CHARACTERS

FATHER DONNELLY: A freshly qualified priest, naive in the ways of the world, yet devout and insightful in his service to the Lord. Recently brought into this parish due to his 'speciality' in dealing with a certain kind of sin.

HEATHER JONES: A retired silver screen actress. Known throughout the world for her portrayal of seductive femme fatales on screen but also her Hollywood sexual exploits. Retiring to this parish has awoken a certain desire in the souls of its in-habitants.

TIME: Rural Ireland in the 90's.

SCENE: *A simple kitchen with a wine rack by the window opposite a kitchen knife set. There are some nice touches that say 'class'. HEATHER JONES enters in high spirits.*

HEATHER. I know it's a funeral and everything, but it doesn't have to be this big downer for every-one. *(Heather moves to the wine rack)* Waaaa waaaa. Sure, if you believe in Heaven, shouldn't it be a celebration?

DONNELLY (O/S). It was a nice sombre affair, Heather. People don't like being brought face to face with death. Especially one of their own.

HEATHER. Ha! One of their own, they wouldn't have anything to do with Jerry only God told them to.

DONNELLY (O/S). I think the correct term is Father McDonald … even though he's dead … I mean … it's still Father, isn't it?

HEATHER. Yes, and I'm sure the townsfolk loved him so much he'll be Saint feckin' McDonald in a few years. What are you doing?

DONNELLY (O/S). I'm getting the wellies off. Wouldn't want to soak the carpets of the great Heather Jones, would I? My Mother would kill me, and Emily would never let me hear the end of it. *(Heather has two glasses of wine in her hand, waiting seductively at the door for Donnelly. He enters in his socks, umbrella under his arm and wellies in hand. He looks at the glasses of wine.)*

DONNELLY. I thought you said tea?

HEATHER. I've no milk.

DONNELLY. I haven't had a drop in …

HEATHER. Are you a pioneer?

DONNELLY. No.

HEATHER. An alcoholic?

DONNELLY. No.

HEATHER. Would you leave a lady to drink on her own?

DONNELLY. No. *(Heather thrusts the wine into his hand and walks away whilst taking a sip of hers. Donnelly struggles with his jacket and the wine glass, places both on the table, then places the jacket on the chair behind him, giving it a rub down.)*

HEATHER. Lovely service all the same, Father. You did well. Must have been very nerve racking up there. All these new faces to you.

DONNELLY. I've been here a month, got to know a lot of people. Emily really helped a lot in getting to know the pari-

HEATHER. A month?

DONNELLY. Mmm. The diocese felt that Gerr- Father McDonald may be on the way out on account of the … *(Donnelly mimes smoking and drinking, indicating Father McDonald did a serious amount of both.)*

DONNELLY. So, I think they planned to have me here to slot right in and keep God's love for his people present in the town. I've got to know quite a lot of people actually. Very friendly. *(He sips his wine.)*

HEATHER. I suppose they're very friendly when they've something to get from you.

DONNELLY. What's that?

HEATHER. Eternal love from the heavenly Father? Everlasting peace, food, forty virgins-

DONNELLY. Think that's the Quran-

HEATHER: -and as much ridin' as a heavenly body can handle.

DONNELLY. Heather Jones. I didn't take you for such a doubting Thomas, nor someone with such a crass tongue.

HEATHER. Father Donnelly, please forgive me. *(Heather stands up, approaches Donnelly and begins to rub his shoulders.)*

HEATHER. I can get quite … passionate when I really care about something. And truth be told, I wouldn't want you to be taken advantage of by any one of a less than reputable character in this town.

DONNELLY. How could they take advantage of me? It's not like I hold the keys to the pearly gates. Nor would I let them.

HEATHER. Let them?

DONNELLY. I'm confident if - and I'm not saying they would - if someone was to try and wrangle their way into heaven through me by deception and stealth and other underhanded manoeuvrings, I'd sniff them out, puff out my chest as a loyal servant of God, and with a quick quip or a- a- witty retort, I'd put an end to their devious tricks. God, I feel like I'm in one of your old Hollywood movies! *(He drinks more wine which Heather is quick to replace.)*

HEATHER. Bit of a fan, are you?

DONNELLY. Well … I must admit, when I was standing over Gerry's- Father McDonald's body saying my prayers, I had a peek at the guest book- book of condolences, and I may have gotten a bit excited that Heather Jones was here. I had heard you retired in a little village in Ireland away from all the hustle and bustle, but I never imagined you'd end up here. Why … in the name of God, did you come back here, Heather?

HEATHER. Love.

DONNELLY. Who is he? I'll show him. *(Donnelly stands and mockingly takes up a fighting stance.)* Remember? Like that line from the film?

HEATHER. My ex-husband. It wouldn't be a fair fight. He's dead. You can dig him up if you like, he's under the floorboards. *(Heather registers the look on Donnelly's face and laughs heartily. Donnelly laughs too, but not as earnestly. He looks to the floorboards. Heather waves him off.)* No. Ya numpty. Laurel Lancaster. I blew his ashes out
over the Nevada desert.

DONNELLY. That was nice, I suppose. Did he request it?

HEATHER. Yes. Out of a cannon actually. A circus

one, this one particular circus cannon. He talked about it for years. 'Heather, when I'm gone, burn me up and shoot me all across the desert but don't shoot me from no namby pamby Chinese-

DONNELLY. Bit racist.

HEATHER. -bullshit cannon Heather, no. The cannon that sent me to Las Vegas in the first place. The cannon I saw in my first circus! Good old American steel. That cannon launched me to my dreams and to the love of my life.'

DONNELLY. Did he fire himself from a cannon?

HEATHER. No, it was-

DONNELLY. Well did he run away with the circus?

HEATHER. No. He was a little boy and his Dad brought him to the circus. One of the best memories of his life, the first time really, he was outside with his family after being sick for most of his childhood. It kind of inspired him to go out into the world … with the force of being launched by a cannon, I guess.

DONNELLY. And did you?

HEATHER. Hmm?

DONNELLY. Did you get the cannon?

HEATHER. Oh yes, I had to.

DONNELLY. Romantic.

HEATHER. They wouldn't release the feckin' money until the cannon was verified to be the real deal. *(Donnelly chuckles.)*

DONNELLY. I suppose you got the last laugh.

HEATHER. The will?

DONNELLY. You got to fire the cannon.

HEATHER. Yeah.

DONNELLY. And love?

HEATHER. I believe I loved him very much.

DONNELLY. No. You said you moved here for love. Was it love of country? Love of peace and quiet? Love of bingo? Which I haven't seen you at yet, by the way. Emily does run a fantastic- *(Heather explodes.)*

HEATHER. He was cheating on me. With another woman. Some culchie whore from, of all places, my Godforsaken Emerald Isle. A little bitch five years my elder, would you believe!

DONNELLY. Heather!

HEATHER. Sorry, Father. *(Heather composes herself, fixes her hair and demurely sits down.)*

HEATHER. It's still a bit raw. He was in love with her, he professed. Love. Bah!

DONNELLY. I'm sorry to hear that. *(Donnelly takes a long drink, she fills his glass again.)*

HEATHER. I gave him everything he wanted, sometimes up to three times a day, for most of the week. *(Donnelly spits the drink out.)*

DONNELLY. What?

HEATHER. Sex. Isn't that what love is? The highest expression two humans can have of it anyway. Sure, what would you know about it?

DONNELLY. Love?

HEATHER. Sex!

DONNELLY. Well … we take a vow of celibacy, but they've recently brought in sex education which is actually quite interesting-

HEATHER. Father. You're a nice man. Lovely. You bring to mind someone who would make a lovely cake jumper for his granny or a big fluffy shoulder to cry on, but you can't talk to me about love if you haven't experienced sex.

DONNELLY. Well, there's no higher love than God has for us. It goes far beyond the physical. You said it yourself - and I'm sorry that your late husband cheated on you, I am, I can't imagine the hurt you felt - but he loved her even though you … ahem … pleasured him three times a day for most of his days. *(Heather stares deathly into Donnelly's eyes.)* Love is more than a simple … pleasure, or a satiated desire. *(Heather continues to stare and Donnelly, now with an empty wine glass, fills it again.)* In no way am I saying you weren't in love or that he didn't love you in … his own way or that you didn't love him. *(He finally notices her death stare.)* Jesus Christ. I should go. *(He takes his jacket and goes to leave.)*

HEATHER. Stay, Father.

DONNELLY. No really, it's getting late, Emily will be worried.

HEATHER. Is she your wife?

DONNELLY. Assistant. 'To help me slot in', she said.

HEATHER. Emily will be fine. She knows you're with me, right?

DONNELLY. Right.

HEATHER. And a Shepherd never leaves its flock when it's in trouble, right?

DONNELLY. Right. What? Are you in trouble?

HEATHER. Moral trouble, Father. Take a seat. I need you to hear my confession. *(Donnelly nods and sits, Heather pours them* another glass of wine.)

HEATHER. I need you to hear my confession. Bless me, Father, for I have sinned. It's been … many decades since my last confession. *(Beat.)* This may take a while. It's trouble of the soul. *(Donnelly blesses her.)*

DONNELLY. Ha! Now this I can handle. Good old-fashioned trouble of the soul. None of this sex scandal and cheating mistresses. God, ha, it's nearly too much for me. Carry on. *(He takes a swig.)*

HEATHER. Should I murder her?

DONNELLY. Murder her? Murder who?

HEATHER. The woman who stole my love from me.

DONNELLY. Ha! Yes, of course! *(Donnelly mimes slitting his throat and hanging himself.)*

HEATHER. I'm serious.

DONNELLY. Yeah. Ha-ha. Of course, you are. *(Donnelly's mirth turns to concern, then confused worry as he starts to gather his things slowly, making to leave.)*

HEATHER. And where do you think you're going?

DONNELLY. To tell the Gards.

HEATHER. To tell the Gards that retired silver screen femme fatale Heather Jones went to confession and is planning a murder in the parish in the back arse of nowhere?

DONNELLY. That is literally what you've just told me.

HEATHER. And you smelling like a winery. *(Donnelly looks at the now empty bottle of wine and is indignant.)* And if word does get out that you're running to the police every time someone confesses something in the blessed sacrament, how will that go down for your beloved flock, huh? What would Emily think of you then?

DONNELLY. You tricked me. *(Heather takes out a cigarette and stares at her prey.)*

HEATHER. So now. The fate of the other woman rests solely in the hands of a rookie priest. Do you feel like you're in one of my movies now?

DONNELLY. Don't somehow twist this on me. If you decide to take a soul, you decide to take a soul … and may your soul be ready for the consequences. And how? How does this rest in my hands?

HEATHER. Ah relax. I haven't murdered anyone … yet. *(Donnelly looks at the floorboards.)* It's a confession, Father. Ever since my husband's death I've been … obsessed. How could he leave me for her? After everything I gave him.

DONNELLY. It's more than just sex, Heather. Love is sacrifice.

HEATHER. Sacrifice? *(Heather explodes again.)* Didn't I sacrifice my body for him at all those sex orgies he dragged me to. The threesomes, the hot sweaty nakedness, every sexual position and thrill you could think of, mashed into one room after another. *(Donnelly blesses himself.)* And he left me. With a letter. *(She takes the letter out of her bra.)*

'Dear Heather, it is with slight regret on my part, but with steadfast conviction, that I must advise, I am leaving you. I no longer desire the worldly delights you have shown me, much of it I am now ashamed of. I have found the real love of my life through electronic communication. Rather than get a divorce and drag it out through the papers and media and such, I have decided to live out my days in a quiet and peaceful cottage with my love, in rural Ireland. I know forgiveness is not in your vocabulary, but please, at the very least, find peace and love in your own heart and be happy, like me. Sincerely, Laurel. Ps ... do not forget the cannon.'

DONNELLY. I know it's painful, but you can't murder the woman, she's innocent.

HEATHER. And wasn't I innocent, giving up my body for him?

DONNELLY. Well ...

HEATHER. No! Of course not, because it was dirty, dirty sex. Isn't

that right, Father? Isn't there one thing you've done that you're ashamed of? You've never had sex?

DONNELLY. No.

HEATHER. You must have masturbated.

DONNELLY. *(Long beat.)* Once.

HEATHER. Once?

DONNELLY. Will it help? *(Heather bursts out laughing.)*

HEATHER. Masturbating?

DONNELLY. *(Embarrassed)* Confessing to you

something I'm ashamed of?

HEATHER. It might.

DONNELLY. There is one thing that springs to mind. We were gardening in the seminary. It was Father O'Boyle's favourite thing to do. Tend to the garden. He was … bent over in the summer heat … I just couldn't fathom how he could never notice his great big builder's arse. I mean, it was like a canyon, didn't he feel a breeze? O'Malley and I would have a chuckle at it, the ridiculousness of it, when one day a frog bounced out of nowhere and straight into my hands. I couldn't believe it. One of God's creatures with no fear in him, just, he had, like a pure trust of us and came to say hello. I showed O'Malley, wanting to share this wonderful moment with him and … he nodded at O'Boyle's arse. *(Beat.)* I knew it was wrong. *(Beat.)* I knew the frog didn't deserve it but the temptation was too much. And I got caught up in the moment and dropped the frog into Father O'Boyle's abyss. *(He cries with shame.)* I've never seen a man his size move so fast.

HEATHER. Hilarious. Still doesn't talk someone down from murder.

DONNELLY. THAT INNOCENT FROG WAS SQUISHED DEAD … and the guilt haunts me to this day.

HEATHER. Didn't you confess?

DONNELLY. Of course, I did. And I felt genuine remorse and I feel I was forgiven, but it still happened, and I still feel guilty when I think about it.

HEATHER. So, if I murder her, all I've got to do is go to confession?

DONNELLY. No. It doesn't work like that. Why, Heather? Why would you throw your life away like that? You said you came back here for love and I thought I was going to hear a happy story.

HEATHER. His love for her, what did she have that I didn't? What did they have that I thought I had?

DONNELLY. The question would drive you mad, Heather.

HEATHER. Yes. Straight to murder. *(There is a pause as Donnelly thinks and Heather sits, resolute in her decision.)*

DONNELLY. Yes of course. Straight to murder. What a lovely little evening you had planned for me.

HEATHER. Yes. There's a grand stretch in the evenings now, isn't there?

DONNELLY. Yes, great drying in that weather.

HEATHER. And not a baby washed in the house.

DONNELLY. Mmm.

HEATHER. Mmm. *(They sit in silence.)*

DONNELLY. Heather-

HEATHER. It would be a crime of passion, Father.

DONNELLY. Crimes of passion only happen in the moment. How long has it been?

HEATHER. Seven years.

DONNELLY. Seven years, Heather? Have the fires of passion not cooled bloody well down at this stage?

HEATHER. Yes, they've turned to ice in fact.

DONNELLY. Have you anything else to confess? We're technically still in confession.

HEATHER. Do you think it'll help?

DONNELLY. Yes, I think so.

HEATHER. Ok. Forgive me, Father, for I have sinned. Where do I start? I have lived a life of what you would consider debauchery. Over -consumption of alcohol, narcotics, I punched a nun in school and spat on my father's face as I ran away to America to be with Laurel. I never wrote home and I barely thought about my parents. I have stolen many things, I have done more than covet a neighbour's wife, if you know what I mean, and whatever else is written on those stone tablets years ago. I moved back to this Godforsaken land to seek out and murder a woman who stole my love from me. My love, who was all I had. The loneliness …

DONNELLY. Go on.

HEATHER. Don't you get the gist?

DONNELLY. The loneliness …

HEATHER. You can't expect me to feel guilty over loneliness. You want me to confess to my loneliness, is that it?

DONNELLY. I think you should confess it to yourself.

HEATHER. *(Long beat.)* This town, Donnelly. It reminds me so much of my home, where I come from, and … all my past exploits have been out in the public eye for years. I see the way the townsfolk look at me. They revile me. They're only short of hissing and throwing holy water on me. Me and Laurel did all those things together. He made everything okay. We were unashamed. I lost belief in God, I lost belief in humanity, truth be told. Laurel and sex were all I had. I could understand if he left me for a younger woman, it would mean my looks have faded and that's it, that's just fucking life but ... an older woman. Older? It wasn't my looks or the

sexuality, it was something else that I didn't have. So, I came here to the town of this other woman to experience this 'love' for myself, but the townsfolk hate me. Why do they hate me? Because I'm not ashamed

of sex? Because I freed myself from the shackles of shame?

DONNELLY. They don't hate you.

HEATHER. How would you know, you're only here a month.

DONNELLY. I just know. *(He smiles at her assuredly. Heather looks up at him expectantly)* Trust me.

HEATHER. Oooohh ... Confession ...

DONNELLY. No!

HEATHER. Tell me!

DONNELLY. I can't, Heather, and you know it.

HEATHER. I'm at my wits end, Father. I need to hear that I'm not really some abomination.

DONNELLY. The confessional is between a person and God.

HEATHER. That everyone has these thoughts.

DONNELLY. It's a sacred, holy place.

HEATHER. That everyone wants threesomes, and

orgies and blowjobs and-

DONNELLY. THERE'S A DISPROPORTIONATE AMOUNT OF MASTURBATION IN THIS VILLAGE. *(Donnelly places his head in his hands, as if he has confessed to a terrible crime. Heather leans back, astonished.)*

HEATHER. What?

DONNELLY. In the supermarket, the car parks, the fields, the butchers, the bakers, the candlestick makers. And not just men, no! The women too!

HEATHER. Ha!

DONNELLY. It's not funny, Heather, it's a crisis. Every day I have to listen to people who I respect in the town, tell me all about running off to a quiet corner and either pulling the plum off themselves or itchin' the bean any time the famous Heather Jones walks by.

HEATHER. Ha!

DONNELLY. I had to write to the bishop.

HEATHER. What did he say?

DONNELLY. He said that masturbation, while sinful, is a sign of a desire to connect with oneself and it's my job to move the desires of the parish to connect with God. That's what it is at its core. And that's what it is with you ... you're the frog.

HEATHER. Excuse me?

DONNELLY. One of God's creatures. Innocent, full of life, just looking to say hello, and you got crushed between your ex-husband's arse cheeks simply because some eejit gave in to his darker impulses. You are looking for love, Heather ... but God is love. You were meant to meet me today. Drop your desire for revenge on this woman and seek real love. In fact, if anyone deserved murder, it was your husband for the years of harmful neglect and manipulation. But not the woman. *(Heather breaks down, cries, and jumps towards Donnelly, hugging him tightly.)*

HEATHER. Do you really think he would have deserved it?

DONNELLY. Yeah. I'm going to go. I would like you to come to church tomorrow and we can discuss your new life and what God's love can mean for you. *(Heather wipes her tears and nods.)*

HEATHER. Okay.

DONNELLY. Okay.

HEATHER. Thank you.

DONNELLY. You're welcome. *(Donnelly heads for the door.)*

HEATHER. Once? *(Donnelly turns.)* You only masturbated once?

DONNELLY. It's a long story. Before I found God's love for me.

HEATHER. Tell me. Before you go. *(Donnelly shifts.)*

HEATHER. I've confessed everything, Father, and I believe we're friends.

DONNELLY. I believe so too.

HEATHER. Once though? *(Laughs.)* What went wrong, didn't you like it?

DONNELLY. It's embarrassing.

HEATHER. Ah, come on. Embarrassing? You literally heard everything I'm about. I'm sure you can give me one embarrassing story.

DONNELLY. I don't think you'll like it.

HEATHER. Try me.

DONNELLY. When I was younger, now we were an incredibly religious household. I mean, when I hit puberty, I asked my Mammy what the hairs on my ... tiddler were for ... and she snapped at me and said don't be so disgusting. So, it just made me very shameful about it, you know? And one day I saw the most beautiful girl in the world. God, I'll never forget it. Something about her eyes, her smile ... it just made me float. I only ever saw her from afar, but I knew I had to have her. And the more I saw her, the more I had this feeling ... you know ... downstairs. I had pictures of her. Hundreds. I'd fantasise every day about her. What she would feel like to touch, to smell, to be around. So ... one day, my Mother was gone out to confession. I knew I had a few hours before she came back so I got Blu Tack and I stuck all the pictures up around my room. I closed my eyes and I just imagined myself in all these scenarios with her. Going for a walk on the pier, her brushing her hair behind her ear and smiling at me, going for date night to the restaurant, the smells, the sounds, her eyes and her smile. Before I knew it, I was touching myself. Playing around you know. I imagined her here with me in my room and I swear, my mind couldn't tell the difference. *(Long beat.)* As I ejaculated, I eventually opened my eyes and my mother- *(beat)* was there at the end of the bed.

HEATHER. What did she do?

DONNELLY. She … tore down the pictures, she started slapping me as I was trying to hide myself with a blanket. She grabbed me by the hair and threw me onto my knees.

HEATHER. That's horrible.

DONNELLY. She stripped the blanket from me, and I was naked. The worse thing was … she … her tears. They were real. She was screaming crying. I must have hurt her so badly. She begged me to pray for forgiveness, so I did. The room was freezing, and I shook. Not from the cold, but from the hurt I caused her. I begged her for forgiveness and promised I'd never do it again. She knelt with me and prayed over her rosary beads for forgiveness for raising such a disgusting son. She did

the full rosary and all I kept saying was 'I'm sorry, I'm sorry'. When she finished the rosary … she just walked out of the room and left me in the dark. I stayed on my knees and I prayed all night. Frozen. The next morning … she wouldn't talk to me. It was like I didn't exist anymore. And then … I was on a bus for the cemetery- seminary. *(Long beat as Donnelly considers his surroundings and history.)* I'm really going to go this time.

HEATHER. Donnelly … who were the pictures of? *(Donnelly gives her a boyish look and has suddenly become extremely shy. Heather moves to him, brushes his hair with her fingers, and kisses him once, softly on the lips.)*

HEATHER. You've nothing to be ashamed of. *(Heather takes Donnelly's collar off. Just as their lips are about to kiss, there is a loud banging on the door, startling Donnelly.)*

DONNELLY. Emily!

HEATHER. That culchie whore! *(Donnelly goes to open the door, while Heather goes to the kitchen and produces a large knife. Donnelly looks over his shoulder. He looks at the knife and then out to where Emily is standing. He puts his arm out, as if calming a bull about to charge. He whispers.)*

DONNELLY. No, Heather. No. I'll be back tomorrow. You're not alone anymore, ok? You're not alone. *(Heather relents, drops her arm, but keeps the knife. Donnelly leaves and closes the door behind him. Heather looks down at the floorboards, then to the door. She looks at the floorboards again and kneels at the place where she joked her husband was buried.)*

HEATHER. You bastard. You fucking bastard. *(She beats pitifully on the floor with the knife. Her bloodlust abated and replaced with grief.)*

THE END

THE BOOK OF KARL

The Book of Karl was first performed at The International Bar, Dublin on March 21st, 2018. The cast was as follows:
Karl Barry McBrien
Bronagh Cherley Kane
Director Luke Corcoran
Stage Designer & Costume Jennifer Keane

CHARACTERS

KARL: A man in his twenties/thirties. Eternally positive, frenetic, and helpful. If he had any friends, they would describe him as a human Labrador puppy. Works at the supermarket, gathering in trolleys and welcoming customers. In this play, he is returning home from a life-changing purchase and is sporting a recent black eye he has covered up with sunglasses.

BRONAGH: Karl's live-in girlfriend. Machiavellian and cutting in her 'humour'. Unemployed and living off Karl's paycheque, she wants to be a writer and is constantly on her laptop/computer.

TIME: Modern day Ireland.

SCENE: *A bedroom with one side of the room unkempt and the other neat and tidy. There are empty whiskey bottles and cigarette cartons strewn around. BRONAGH is on her laptop on the bed, legs crossed, video- calling someone.*

BRONAGH. No, no, no I wasn't saying that, honey. No. Not at all, sweetheart, that's not what I meant. *(She smiles broadly.)* You know I forgive you for all that. It's nothing now. Water under the bridge. Yes. Today? *(Worried.)* Will you do it today? Wonderful! *(She claps her hands in delight.)* Oh? But you're in the supermarket, I can't! *(She gets shy.)* No. No. *(She gets scared, but then quickly covers it with a smile and a laugh.)* Okay. Okay … you want to see them again … *(She slowly pulls her top up to underneath her breasts. KARL enters the room, and she slams the laptop closed.)*

KARL. Honey! I'm home! *(Karl looks at the laptop that's just closed with Bronagh leaning over it.)* Finished writing for the day? I can't wait for the novel to be finished. *(Karl is carrying two bags of groceries, he awkwardly leans in to kiss Bronagh, who* *turns her head, ever so slightly, to avoid the lips. Karl is completely unperturbed and smiles, delighted with 'the kiss', and continues to unpack the groceries.)* What a day. The local gang of 'howayaz' … oh, sorry! Offensive language. Stole the shopping trolleys. Mickah wouldn't let me clock out until I got them all back, he said "what kind of a fucking trolley attendant loses the trolleys?" I said "well, it's not really my responsibility if they get stolen from me, is it?", and he just repeated himself. So … message received! I had to go into the council estates and get them back. I had to negotiate with all these youngfellas. It was like something out of 'Mad Max'. One of them, it was like they made an effigy of the trolley. So, I strolled up to him in me Hi-Viz, you know. Most youngfellas just ran when they seen it. Thinking I was an authority figure or something. Which, I am, of course. So, I said to him "Oi! Youngfella! Do you know who that trolley belongs to?"

BRONAGH. What did they say? *(He takes off his sunglasses to reveal a huge black eye on the left side of his face.)*

KARL. They called me a 'big spa' and get the 'F' out of here before they shove the trolley up me hoop-

BRONAGH. No. What did work say about your accident?

KARL. What accident? *(Bronagh gets off the bed and goes towards Karl, touches his face.)*

BRONAGH. About your accident, sweetheart. Remember? When you were clumsy? *(She kisses his* *black eye, which makes Karl wince, but he cannot bear to let go of this affection from Bronagh.)*

KARL. Oh no, no, no, no, I've sorted that. Yeah. I wore the glasses anyway and … great suggestion by the way, you're so clever. I just said I had a clumsy accident at home … you know?

BRONAGH. Which is the truth.

KARL. Which is the truth. So, this morning I went in and Mickah actually got a promotion. Do you remember him from the Christmas party last year? You got on well. I'm so glad my girlfriend likes my friends.

BRONAGH. Mickah's your friend now?

KARL. Well … colleague … work … work colleague … friend. He does like to play jokes on me, aw yeah, put Karl in a box and put him up the escalator, wrap him in pallet wrap. But … as it turns out … he got a promotion in work and he's now my boss. I'm so happy for him.

BRONAGH. That's wonderful. Fair play to him, I always knew there was something about him.

KARL. Yeah. So, I took off my glasses and said "look boss, don't be worried, there's nothing to be alarmed about here now, okay? I just had a clumsy accident at home, that's all." *(Bronagh is getting very impatient.)*

BRONAGH. And what did he say?

KARL. He said "So? Get out there and look after them trolleys as if they were your new-born babies." Typical Mickah. *(Bronagh is suddenly angry and leaves Karl's embrace, just as he is moving in for a* *kiss.)*

KARL. What? Was it something I said?

BRONAGH. Nothing. It's fine.

KARL. No, no, no. It was, it was something I said. Trolleys. Mickah. Babies. *(Bronagh shoots him a dagger.)* Oh, I'm so sorry, bab- honey. Sweetheart. I should have known. I mean, I do know, I'm sorry-

BRONAGH. Oh, you do know? So, you just mention it on purpose to hurt me, is that it?

KARL. No, I didn't do it on purpose, please. *(Karl cowers, goes to the groceries and produces a bottle of whiskey and two packets of cigarettes.)*

BRONAGH. You know how much I hate babies.

KARL. I know. I'm sorry.

BRONAGH. The crying. The neediness. God, they're just so fuckin' needy. What's the point in them like? *(She takes the bottle of whiskey.)*

KARL. Totally. The smelly nappies, all that stuff horrible. You're right, I shouldn't have said anything.

BRONAGH. You should know, sweetheart, the mere mention of the word drives me insane. You know that now, right? *(She walks to Karl and places her hand on his testicles.)*

KARL. I do.

BRONAGH. So, don't mention them again, right?

KARL. I won't. I won't. *(She squeezes sharply but gently enough to get a whimper.)*

BRONAGH. Good lad. *(She kisses him on the lips.)* You know I love you though, right? *(She smacks his face playfully and walks away.)*

KARL. I love you too. *(Karl gets a glass for Bronagh, who pours herself a double and him a single.)* So? How is the novel coming on? Did you get past the dreaded page 4? *(Bronagh shoots him a look.)*

KARL. You know, the one you're stuck on and you can't seem to get over? I can't wait to see what's written after that page, once you get past that hump. I'm so proud of you. Do you want a back rub?

BRONAGH. I'm going out tonight.

KARL. Great. With who?

BRONAGH. A friend. Something wrong with that? I can't have my own alone time? God, you're so suffocating sometimes.

KARL. Of course, alone time, of course. No, absolutely, it's just … I have something I wanted to share with you. I thought I'd wait 'til after one or two … you know, *(to himself)* when you become friendlier, *(to Bronagh)* but if you're going out, we can do it now.

BRONAGH. Did you get me a gift? *(Karl looks at the whiskey and the cigarettes.)*

KARL. Well … em … this … this is something very special and dear to me.

BRONAGH. You're not gonna show me your childhood teddy and talk about your mother and cry again, are you?

KARL. No. No. No. It's not Brucie, he's locked away somewhere special now, isn't he? You're keeping him safe for me and I appreciate that. This is something different. You know the way I like the star signs, the horoscopes and the, you know, wacky spiritual stuff?

BRONAGH. Tell me about it.

KARL. Well l … this … is a book. *(Karl takes out a pink fluffy book that is full of pages. It is handwritten and scruffy.)*

BRONAGH. It looks like a homeless drag queen's diary.

KARL. He wasn't homeless. He was travelling through-

BRONAGH. You robbed a traveller's diary?

KARL. No, I bought it. And he wasn't a member of the travelling community, he was a druid. *(Bronagh laughs with derision.)*

BRONAGH. He must have seen you coming.

KARL. Oh my God!

BRONAGH. What?

KARL. That is EXACTLY what he said. How on earth did you know that?

BRONAGH. I know everything. You know that. *(Karl waves his finger at her, impressed.)*

KARL. He walked up to me when I was negotiating with the youngfellas. The trolley was on this bonfire in this old playground. There was youngfellas and youngones all dotted around like they were trying to sacrifice the trolley to the ancient Gods or something. It was all a bit mad really. Like something out of a Cuchulainn story or something. So … Franko … the leader of this particular tribe, who I was negotiating with for the return of the trolley, was walking towards me quite angrily, probably because he couldn't hear me or something, and I wasn't respecting his disability or something, he got very close and was about to say- no, shout something when he stopped … and I saw pure fear in his eyes. I said "now, now, Franco, there's no need to be afraid, I'm just here to talk" but he ran off and all the others disappeared too. It was eerily quiet except from the flames from the trolley. I turned around and there was this druid standing over my shoulder. *(Bronagh leans in, suddenly interested.)*

BRONAGH. What did he say?

KARL. "Hey man." *(Bronagh gives a sigh of exasperation. She has been drinking at this stage and is more amenable than we have seen her.)*

KARL. Oh, right so. So, he said … "I have seen you coming in my dreams." Which I thought was a bit sexual … and I was thinking, I'm gonna have to let him down gently, kind of like, 'look pal, I have a girlfriend at home' *(he looks at Bronagh).* A beautiful girlfriend, the love of my life, my soul mate.

BRONAGH. Continue the story.

KARL. So, he says to me, "you probably thought that was a bit sexual, didn't you?" and I was amazed. He read my mind. And then he said something incredibly weird, but also true … He said "everything you've ever done in your life has led you here. Yes. Right here. All your hopes, all your dreams, your childhood, your teenage years, your parents, your choices, your victories, your defeats, everything, all included in your entire life, has led you here. Right here. To this very moment." *(Beat.)* Isn't that mad? Everything we've ever done in our lives has led us to each other?

BRONAGH. So? Everyone knows that. It's not some divine providence or anything. There's no reason to it.

KARL. But it gives everything a reason, doesn't it? There's a reason why we're here. And on that note. He produced this book. *(He waves the fluffy book around and throws it to Bronagh on the bed, who flicks through the pages quickly, then drops it.)*

BRONAGH. It's handwritten? It's all gobbledegook.

KARL. Yeah, that's the point. He said this book is for me. It has been passed down generation to generation and now it's my turn.

BRONAGH. How much did he charge you?

KARL. Let me tell you how to use the book first. It's fascinating.

BRONAGH. How much?

KARL. He said, "it'll cost you everything." I said, "well I've only my two euro seventy for the bus and a coupon for a chicken roll for my lunch." And he said, "that'll do" and handed me the book.

BRONAGH. You didn't eat lunch?

KARL. Too excited.

BRONAGH. Well, I'm not feeding you. You know I hate cooking. I told you that before I moved in here.

KARL. Yeah no, no, no it's fine. I'll make a sandwich later. Anyway ... *(Bronagh is now disinterested and is working away on her laptop.)* To use the

book. He said, based on the principle that everything in your life, every single minute detail and atom of your existence in your past has led you here … to use the book … *(he holds the book in his hands).* Close your eyes and take a deep breath in *(he breaths in).* Flick through the pages *(he flicks through).* And with your left hand, because it's closest to your heart, put your index finger down. Open your eyes. And whatever sentence you land on is exactly what you need to hear in your life, exactly at that point. *(He reads the book.)* 'She's cheating on you with your boss.' *(Bronagh looks like a deer in the headlights. Karl slowly turns to face her.)* Mickah? My boss. In the supermarket? You said nothing happened at the Christmas party.

BRONAGH. Nothing did happen. Why are you bringing this up now? We've been over this and over this.

KARL. We only spoke about this once. I saw the photo you were tagged in with him where you were kissing each other.

BRONAGH. He kissed me. You know this already; the camera just caught that exact moment. *(Karl almost agrees, figuring this out.)*

KARL. He asked for a kiss on the cheek and then turned his head at the exact moment you were going to kiss him and that's what the camera caught. It was nothing. Nothing to worry about.

BRONAGH. Yeah, see? Nothing to worry about. I think it's sweet that you think I'd find you worthy of cheating on.

KARL. Worthy?

BRONAGH. Yes. If I wanted someone else, I'd just be with someone else. I mean look at me and look at you. You hit the jackpot here, wouldn't you say?

KARL. Yeah, but the book …

BRONAGH. Oh, you're gonna believe a poxy fucking book over me now, is it? Are you calling me a fucking liar, is that it? *(Bronagh walks up menacingly to Karl, who flinches.)*

KARL. No, no, no. *(Bronagh's phone rings, they are both frozen. Bronagh gives Karl daggers and answers the phone in a sickly-sweet voice.)*

BRONAGH. Hello, honey, how are you? I believe congratulations are in order? Yes, twenty minutes, lovely. Just getting warmed up here. *(Bronagh takes a swig of her whiskey. Karl is suspicious and goes to the book again, doing the ritual.)* Oh, yes. The special one. OK. Just ring the buzzer when you're downstairs and I'll come out to you. Woooo! *(She laughs and hangs up)* I've to get ready. *(She leaves. Karl has his finger on the book.)*

KARL. *(Reads.)* 'The answer you seek you have already found.' *(To Bronagh.)* Who was that on the phone?

BRONAGH. My friend.

KARL. What are you celebrating?

BRONAGH. A promotion.

KARL. Bronagh, is that Mickah? Are you celebrating his promotion? Tell me now if you're cheating on me with each other.

BRONAGH. Why all this talk about fucking cheating, huh? Are you cheating on me, is that it? Trying to guilt-trip me because I'm going out with a friend? You can't let me have a life. You have a job whilst I'm couped up here all day. You think I like sitting around the house, waiting on you hand and foot when you come home. Listening to your bullshit and having you throw accusations like this at me. *(She starts crying.)* You know I hate asking you for money but I've no way of supporting myself until my novel is published. You just don't believe in me while I pour my heart out into that computer. Do you know how difficult it is? No and you don't care. Do you?

KARL. Of course, I care.

BRONAGH. No, you don't, you just accuse me of cheating on you because you want to guilt me into staying at home. You will probably try tell me you don't have any money now because you spent it on that fucking book.

KARL. I don't.

BRONAGH. I knew it. I fucking knew it. Fine, I'll stay here and be your little slave, is that what you want? *(Bronagh sits down, dejected.)*

BRONAGH. Just keep me here, ply me with drink, keep me drunk ... too drunk to do anything with my life. *(She drinks more viciously.)*

KARL. No. Look. I'm sorry, don't get upset. I'm sorry for accusing you. Here, I have money hidden. *(She sobs and drinks more. Karl goes to the edge of the stage to a secret hiding space where he takes out some cash and puts the rest back. Bronagh, through tears,*

has a look around him to the hiding place.)
KARL. Here. Is twenty OK?
BRONAGH. Forty. *(Karl hands it over and she wipes her tears. He kisses her forehead. Bronagh gets up and goes off stage.)*
KARL. Where are you going?
BRONAGH. To have a shower and get changed. *(Karl sits on the bed, worried. He looks at the phone. He looks at the book. He starts to cry. He does the ritual.)*
KARL. 'Help is available for you, but you must be open to trust.' *(He does the ritual again and we can hear a noise of a shower in the background.)* 'You are severely wounded and it's OK to use the book as a crutch, for now.' *(He does the ritual again.)* 'True understanding is not of the mind, but of the heart.' *(He does the ritual.)* 'That which is not truly understood, will repeat itself until it is.' *(To himself.)* But what do I have to understand? *(He does the ritual.)* 'Sorrow and yourself.' *(To himself.)* Bronagh means sorrow in Irish. Oh … okay … I have to understand her. I got you. *(He does the ritual. The shower turns off.)* 'You can only understand someone else as deep as you understand yourself.' *(To the book.)* But what do I do? Tell me what to do? *(He does the ritual, Bronagh returns and starts getting dressed.)* 'Allow me'. Okay … Okay … Bronagh … my love … I think I understand you now. With the help of this book, I am going to figure out both of us and it'll make us both happier in the end.
BRONAGH. Still with that book? *(Karl happily does*

the ritual.)

KARL. 'Take your shit and leave.' *(Bronagh turns slowly. Karl panics and puts his finger on the books pages frenetically.)* 'Stay the course, friend.' *(He flicks through the book.)* 'It's for the betterment of both of you.'

BRONAGH. What did you say to me?

KARL. Stay strong.

BRONAGH. About getting my shit and leaving? *(Karl does the ritual.)*

KARL. 'Trust me and let me speak.' Fine. *(Karl does the ritual quicker with every sentence now, letting the words flow out of him.)*

KARL. Not only are you no good for me. We are no good for each other. 'It's toxic.' Toxic? That's a strong word.

BRONAGH. Toxic?

KARL. I know! I wouldn't have said that!

BRONAGH. You think I'm toxic and you want me to leave you? You're dumping me? And what would you do without me? Hmm? *(Karl does the ritual.)*

KARL. 'Grow.'

BRONAGH. Grow? Oh?? So, I'm stopping you now, is it? Stopping you from growing? Fine. Fuck you, you little weasel. After everything I've ever done for you. *(Bronagh packs up all her stuff.)* You want me gone. I'm fucking gone. Out of your life forever. You know you're gonna end up so alone without me. Where are you gonna get a woman like me? A snivelling little wretch like you … so needy all the time anyway. Grow? Ha! I'm going to do the growing. I fucking hate you. *(Karl is torn but goes to the book again.)*

KARL. 'If you find yourself hating something, it is because a part of you is the forgotten inverse of the thing you hate.'

BRONAGH. Oh. You think I'm just like you. A coward who can't even speak for himself. Using a poxy book to break my heart. *(She sobs. Karl goes to the book.)*

KARL. 'Your heart was broken long before we met.'

BRONAGH. Fuck you. Get out of my fucking way. *(Bronagh gathers up her stuff into a big bag.)*

KARL. Who's coming to pick you up? It's Mickah, isn't it? *(Bronagh screams.)*

BRONAGH. Yes. Of course it is. You fucking moron. Think you're so clever figuring that out on your own without your precious book. He's gonna be so happy to be with me now. Not having to hide anything. Slinking around the back of you. God I should have left you long ago. *(Karl starts to cry and sits down, head in his knees.)*

BRONAGH. Starting to cry now? Man up.

KARL. What, you can cry but I can't? How is that fair?

BRONAGH. You're supposed to be a man. This is your decision remember? You asked me to 'get my shit and leave.' Well, I'm going. And look who's crying? Pathetic.

KARL. Why are you like this? Why can't you just be nice? That's all I've ever wanted, is to just have someone be nice to me. *(Bronagh laughs and sits* *down on the chair and pours another whiskey.)*

KARL. Why are you just sitting there? You said you were leaving.

BRONAGH. I'm just waiting on Mickah with the big dickah to pick
me up. And I'm enjoying this. No more hiding. It's out in the open. Oh … that book is magical indeed. *(Karl does the ritual.)*

KARL. 'What happened to you when you were a baby?'

BRONAGH. What? *(Karl does the ritual.)*

KARL. 'No more hiding.'

BRONAGH. I've nothing to hide. *(Karl does the ritual.)*

KARL. 'Then speak.'

BRONAGH. No. I'm not speaking about my child-hood. I don't need to. Unlike you, Karl. When you went to that therapist and all he kept saying to you was, 'leave Bronagh.' Yeah, like I was all the source of your fucked up mental illness. You remember what you told me about your mother? How she used to belittle you with words. Oh, boo-hoo. Little words. Sticks and fucking stones. You know why she belittled you? Because you deserved it. Yeah. That's it, you were probably so needy and clingy all the time, maybe crying out in the night scared … like a little fuckin snotty whinge-bag. I bet your mom still came and picked you up and didn't leave you there screaming. I bet your mom took an inter-est in your school essays and didn't burn them in front of you and make you do them again because of a spelling mistake when you were four. I bet your mom didn't beat you regularly or even worse, irregularly, for any fucking whim she had, but mine did. I bet she didn't call you into the sitting room in the middle of the night and burn you with cigarettes? And you know what? She was right. I deserved it. It made me strong. And you have the audacity to go to therapy and blame it all on your mother. You make me sick. *(Karl does the ritual.)*

KARL. 'By projecting your pain, you make yourself sick.' *(Bronagh sits in silence. She then stands up, grabbing the book. She does the ritual.)*

BRONAGH. 'Put me down now.' *(She slams the book on the floor, goes to stamp on it whilst Karl puts his hand out to grab the book, Bronagh stamping on his hand instead. He shouts in pain.)*

BRONAGH. Oh look, another clumsy accident. Fuck this, I'm calling Mickah. *(She takes out her phone and Karl notices something under the bed. Karl sighs with sadness and does the ritual with an injured hand.)*

KARL. 'Tell her about Brucie'. You're right. My mam only beat me once. Everything else was lovely. It was my birthday, and I was in the living room dancing to a Michael Jackson tape she bought me. Thriller. *(He mimes the dance. Bronagh hangs up and starts listening.)* I learned the dance and I was practising because I wanted to show her. I called her as I was practising. "Mam" I called out. "Mam." I was dancing when she came in and the look on her face was one of rage. It was like she was possessed. I didn't know at that time what rage was ... and she calmly picked me by the back of the head and smashed my face into the tape deck and knocked me out. I didn't feel anything until I woke up in the hospital and the nurse gave me an ice-cream. My mam came in, flanked by two doctors. She was in a hospital gown. She said that she was so sorry, but she was sick. She was ill. And sometimes she does mean things because of voices in her head. They tell her to do bad stuff and sometimes they win. But it's not really her and it wasn't really her that hurt me, but she was still so sorry. And she had to go away so that the doctors could help her. So, she gave me Brucie so I could always remember the good side of her. And I gave you Brucie to mind ... *(Karl reaches under Bronagh's bed and pulls out a severely charred and damaged Teddy Bear. Bronagh's face is one of guilt and shock.)* And look what you did to him. Look. *(She runs and hugs Karl, almost childlike.)*

BRONAGH. I'm sorry Karl. I'm so sorry. I need help. I need help. *(Karl accepts the hug, it's all he's ever wanted. He steels himself and frees himself from her clutches.)*

KARL. No. No more. Get out. Get out! *(Shocked by the force of Karl's voice, Bronagh leaves, and Karl is kept in his grief.)* Oh God. I can't - what do I do now? What do I do now? *(He collapses on the chair, takes a drink and does the ritual.)* All you ever needed was time, truth and tears. *(He does the ritual.)* You'll be okay, son. *(He does the ritual.)* There's no love like your mother has for you. *(He strokes Brucie and cries, dropping the book. Every page is blank.)*

THE END

JOBBER

JOBBER was first performed at The International Bar, Dublin on
March 21st, 2018. The cast was as follows:
Dar Jason Deeney
Finbarr Padraig McGinley
Director Luke Corcoran
Stage Designer & Costume Jennifer Keane

CHARACTERS

DAR: (20+) A working class 'lad's lad' and yet,
a 'mummy's boy'. Having spent several years
on social welfare, he is astute in his know-
ledge of contract and employment law; knowing exactly what he is entitled to.

FINBARR (BAR): (50+) Dar's father. Polite, conscientious, and all too aware that he is a product of a different era. Society has moved on at such a fast pace for Finbarr that he has decided 'if you can't beat 'em, join 'em'.

TIME: Ireland, 2030

SCENE: *As close to a doctor's office as possible. There is a washbasin on the right-hand side. There are privacy curtains, which can be used to box off one side of the stage. There is a chair facing the audience and one chair with its back to the audience. DAR enters in high spirits with a briefcase under his arm, wearing a suit, an overcoat, and a hat. He is holding a mobile phone in front of him that is attached to a small tripod or gimbal.*

DAR. Hi Mum! Just leaving you another video message. How did the treatment go? Studies have shown that the symptoms can be, if not reversed, totally eradicated after a couple of sessions. That's why it's so expensive. So, me and Julie - she's such a great girlfriend, honestly can't wait for you to meet her. We decided that we would get an extra job each to pay for the treatment. Don't thank me yet. We've still a ways to go but I'm after landing this fantastic evening job. Really flexible hours. It was actually Julie that found it. She was gonna do it, but she types all day, so she's got that carpal tunnel syndrome thing going on. We're looking into suing the company and seeing if they were in any way negligent about it. You see for claims to be successful; you need *(he sets the phone and tripod down and washes his hands in a handbasin.)* a duty of care between employer and employee, which every employer assumes automatically. *(He turns his back on the phone as he dries his hands and applies hand sanitizer to it.)* Negligence. Or to prove negligence. Like, we will need to prove that Julie's carpal tunnel syndrome was an avoidable consequence of the job and finally … *(he sits down, opens the briefcase and takes out a makeup kit and various colours of nail polish. He lines them up, symmetrically examining all of them.)* damage. Someone has had to suffer damage for there to be a successful claim. Pity you can't sue anyone for cancer. I guess I could try suing God, if anyone would give it a fair whack, I would, for the damage He caused you. But look, don't worry. The treatment, it's experimental right now in Ireland, about time they legalized it for f-look, it'll work out. If you fight something enough, it eventually turns out your way. Like this job, actually, funny story about how I got it. They saw Julie's social media page and reached out to get in touch, told her what it would entail but she had to disclose any medical conditions. Fair enough I suppose, proper order really. So, Julie declined and said, "but I've got someone who could take my place instead." *(Dar examines the doctor's curtain, gives it a quick rub down with a sponge and dries it).* So, they were like "yeah definitely, we'd love to meet them for an interview", so she tells me about the job, shows me the rate of pay - fantastic commission structure by the way, you can earn up to three times your standard rate in the evenings and weekends. Great stuff, I say. Sign me up. So, I get there, dressed all smart for the interview like you taught me when I was younger. 'Clothes make the man' and I was like "hello, I'm here for the interview" and they were like, "ehhh" and I was like "Julie? Recommended by Julie, you said you were very interested?" And they were like … (*Dar pulls the curtain across revealing a glory hole cut into one of the curtains, dividing the stage in two, essentially making his 'office' complete.*) "But you're a man." And I was like "Oh? Because I'm a man, I can't work here, is that it? (*He starts to paint his fingernails with the nail polish, taking meticulous care.*) Need I remind you of the Employment Equality Act 1998, which out-laws discrimination in a wide range of employment areas. This legislation defines discrimination as treating one person in a less than favourable fashion than another person, based on any one of nine grounds, including … gender." So, they were a bit stunned, and I asked if they wanted me to name the other eight, which I could. (*Dar inhales and on the exhale, nonchalantly rhymes off the other eight.*) Civil status, family status, sexual orientation, religion, age, disability, race and membership of the traveller community. So, I said "may I remind you that you were going to offer my co-habitant Julie a job, were you not?" And they were like, "yes", and I was like "so, Julie has managed to find you a replacement and suddenly, you are not satisfied. A person's gender has absolutely no bearing on their ability to do any job, especially if that person is ready, willing, and able, which I am. If you're telling me, you're not going to let me work here based on my gender, how about I walk straight out of this office and into my very competent and busy solicitor's office and we'll see what they have to say on the matter, hmm?" (*He continues to paint his nails.*) Needless to say, Mum, they weren't slow about handing me my own office and signing a contract there and then. Never let it be said that Eileen O'Hara raised a slouch for a son. I could have still gone to the solicitors, Mum, but it's a new industry still finding its feet so I'm prepared to let it slide ... for now. *(Dar hears someone enter off stage. He whispers now.)* Ok, Mum. First client of the night. Gotta go. *(He makes a kissing sound with his lips then puts his attention on the client. He sticks his head through the hole in the partition.)* Howaya! Come on in. *(He pats the chair.)* Down you come. Relax. *(Dar hands the client a baby wipe.)* Wipe. *(Dar takes the baby wipe and drops it into the bin.)* Ready? *(Dar sticks his arm through the glory hole and administers a hand job to the client. After a few seconds he checks his watch and speaks to the audience as he 'works'.)* It's really not that bad a job to be honest. Minimal manual labour and, to be fair, I think the clients are just on the cusp of ... a release. Which is what it this is. Look, we all have needs. Ever heard of Maslow's hierarchy of needs? Self-actualisation, esteem, love and belonging, safety and lastly, physiological. Which is the need you are seeing being fulfilled right here. *(He examines the fruits of his labour through the hole.)* There's nothing to it. Julie doesn't mind at all; she knows I need the money for my mother and she's incredibly supportive. Do I think it's cheating? No. Not at all. Women come in here too, ya know. Sure, the French president says she can't start the day without a good climax. Sets her up for the morning. Sure, how else is she supposed to deal with such a high-pressure job? I've lots of clients. Since they legalised certain aspects of the sex trade, I voted yes by the way, business in the 'Wanktuary' has been booming. Clients on lunch, before work, after work. I can see a definite uplift around the city now. People are a lot calmer. It's intimacy without

the intimac- *(his client has 'finished'.)* Oh. Grand job. *(Dar hands his client a wipe, examines him and hands him another; takes his credit card and puts it against his phone, making a 'beep' noise.)* Ok, thank you very much. *(He hands back the card.)* See you next week. Don't be afraid to fill out our front desk questionnaire! *(He turns to the audience.)* They give me a bonus based on my client's feedback. On a good evening, the boss said I might turn over twenty-five clients. What's the busiest day? Monday morning, actually. Did you know most heart attacks worldwide occur in the early hours of Monday morning? People are getting up to go to jobs they hate, in cars they can't afford, to come home to a house they'll never own. I calculate I must have saved at least fifteen lives doing this job. So yeah. I am proud of my work I'd say. After twelve weeks, they give you your level six Q.Q.I. *(FINBARR enters the stage with trepidation.)*

FINBARR. Eh … hello? *(Finbarr moves around the room taking his coat off. He hasn't spotted the glory hole yet. Dar notices his new client and panics. He closes shut the glory hole and we can see him squirm in panic.)*

FINBARR. Hello? *(Dar covers his mouth with a fresh baby wipe and talks through it, muffling his voice and attempting to hide it with a French accent.)*

DAR. No.

FINBARR. No, what?

DAR. Closed. We are closed.

FINBARR. Closed? They sent me down here. They said all the other

rooms were busy and this one was free.

DAR. No.

FINBARR. No? Listen sonny, I have a coupon! *(Finbarr takes a coupon out of his wallet.)* And if you don't honour this coupon, I'll go straight … to … the front desk and I'll leave a … a … one star review in the questionnaire. *(There is a tense standoff between the two.)* I'm going. *(Even more tense as Finbarr takes a step, making sure his step is heard.)* One. *(Dar shakes.)* Two. *(Dar, throwing a strop, sticks his head out the glory hole.)*

DAR. DAD!

FINBARR. Son?

DAR. WHAT- ARE YOU DOING HERE?

FINBARR. Wh- wh- wh-

DAR. What are you doing here?

FINBARR. What am I doing here? What are you doing here?

DAR. I work here.

FINBARR. Oh God. You work here?

DAR. Yes! Earning that extra money for Mum. Who you should be at home with, looking after!

FINBARR. Lookin' after? Says the man who hasn't been home in weeks! I have been looking after her.

DAR. Oh yeah? So, you just decided to come out here for a hand shandy? *(Finbarr bursts into tears and sits down, distraught.)*

FINBARR. I knew this was a bad idea. I knew it. The internet said this was the hottest start-up in Dublin and I thought … you know what Finbarr, you've been through the years, never once trying out these fads … Tamagotchis, avocado toast, spidget finners and now the jobbing stations popped up in the area, I thought I'd give it a go. The article said it's so many health benefits … supposed to prevent heart attacks. It's hard to get my head around all these fads. The world just moves too quick for me, I think. The one thing I looked forward to all month-

DAR. All month? Would you not just do the job yourself?

FINBARR. Never have I ever masturbated whilst I've been married to your mother. It just seems like cheating.

DAR. And isn't going to a jobbing station cheating? *(Finbarr drops his head in guilt, but then lifts it up when he realizes something.)*

FINBARR. Julie! And what about Julie? Does Julie know what you're doing here? Masturbating random men!

DAR. And women!

FINBARR. Oh yes, you wouldn't possibly discriminate on gender! Does she know what you're doing?

DAR. Yes! They offered her the job first actually and I took it instead.

FINBARR. Oh God. Am I just so out of touch that I don't understand any of this?

DAR. But you were looking to give it a go?

FINBARR. Your mother asked me to give it a go. Dar, she's no energy, it's all spent fighting that feckin' disease. I didn't want to come here. I'd rather her and I did it again. I don't care that she's got cancer, she still has needs. Have you ever heard of Maslow's hierarchy of needs?

DAR. Of course, I have.

FINBARR. Well, I wanted to make sure all your mother's needs are being fulfilled. But she told me … that I can't look after her if I'm not looking after myself. She knew we hadn't had sex in a while. Even when she's dying on that bed at home … she wants me to be ok. Me? She asked me to try something new. She knows I never partook in any of them fads … and she cut this coupon out of an old school magazine. She said it's supposed to be very good.

DAR. Our clients do have a high satisfaction rating and the higher the satisfaction rating, the higher the commission I get … *(Finbarr leaps out of his chair.)*

FINBARR. That's my boy! Always looking to be the best, make the most out of any job, always looking for that number one spot.

DAR. Yeah, so the more jobs I do, the more money I can get for Mum's treatment.

FINBARR. How much is one session here?

DAR. Thirty-five euro.

FINBARR. And how much is the treatment?

DAR. Fifty thousand euro.

FINBARR. Fifty thousand? You'll have to wank off a million men.

DAR. And women.

FINBARR. And women.

DAR. One thousand four hundred and twenty-eight point five clients.

FINBARR. And how many have you done so far?

DAR. Twenty. Twenty-one including your coupon, thank you very much. *(He takes the coupon and puts it against his phone which makes a beeping sound.)*

FINBARR. It'll take years to raise that money, Dar, and I don't think … I don't think … your mother has that much time left.

DAR. If anyone can hit that target, it's me, Dad.

FINBARR. I know you can, son. I know you can. *(Finbarr takes the chair and turns it around, sitting at the back of the stage.)*

FINBARR. My son. Always so good with numbers. Contract law. Do you remember that time the builder came round and burst the boiler and flooded the downstairs?

DAR. You were still gonna pay him, you basket case.

FINBARR. I didn't want to make a fuss. I liked the quiet life, Dar … but you … you looked up the builder's insurance company and asked for a copy of their insurance policy in black and white. Posted to you.

DAR. I know they had to by law if I requested it.

FINBARR. They did away with post by that stage. They couriered the contract out to you. A sixteen-year-old standing at the door with his arms crossed, ready to give the delivery driver a bollocking if he was late. But my son gave him one anyway. *(Father and son laugh at the memory.)* You were always braver than me in a lot of ways kid, smarter too, more friends than I can imagine. But this, Dar … trying to raise money for your mother … we've been over and over the treatment options.

DAR. But we haven't tried this one yet. Cannabis treatment is the newest thing, it's a big success in America and if we can get the money for her, maybe you can help around here too.

FINBARR. Is that the treatment? Cannabis?

DAR. It's why I've been working here.

FINBARR. Do you remember your sixteenth birthday?

DAR. Yeah, you and Mum put up the canopy out the back.

FINBARR. And all your friends were there, and Ciaran brought that
stuff. The scoobie doobie whatever …

DAR. Yes, dad.

FINBARR. And you offered me some, but those fads really aren't for me you know. But your mum … always up for trying something new. Even for me. (*He gestures around the room to emphasise his point.*) And she tried some … and went green as a ghost, remember?

DAR. She got the greenies dad, it's normal.

FINBARR. And I was worried and I took her to the hospital but you told me not to, that I was worrying too much and that she'd be fine … but when I got there, she went into shock … they did tests, they've been doing them for years in the former United States … and they found that your mother is one of a very, very, very, rare breed of people in the world that react negatively to any cannabinoid in their system.

DAR. That's bollox.

FINBARR. It's true.

DAR. No. You told me she just got the greenies and she was fine, there was nothing to worry about.

FINBARR. I WASN'T GOING TO TELL MY SIX-TEEN-YEAR-OLD SON THAT HE NEARLY KILLED HIS MOTHER. (*There is a stunned silence as both are taken aback by the ferocity of the outburst.*) I'm sorry. (*There is a pause as Dar sulks after being scolded.*) Anaphylaxis. That's what they called it. It's very rare but it's possible … Dar, you've been out of the house since your mother got the diagnosis of c-

DAR. Don't say it.

FINBARR. Cancer. I'm saying it and I'll say it again. Cancer. Will you please, instead of sending all these video messages, come home and see her with your own eyes?

DAR. I have to try. You might be here trying to 'take a break' from looking after Mum but I'm here … jobbing … to try and get her better.

FINBARR. You haven't seen her once!

DAR. I send a video once a day.

FINBARR. Son, it's not the same as seeing her face to face and getting to grips with reality.

DAR. Actually, technology has gotten so good that it's just like being in the same room as someone.

FINBARR. Just come home, son. The cannabis is a no-go. It's … what would you call it? A failed venture, and that's ok. You tried. Just come home and at least hold your mother's hand.

DAR. I'm not giving in so easily. I'm gonna stay here, earn as much money as possible and figure something out.

FINBARR. We don't need the money!

DAR. No, we need a cure!

FINBARR. We've tried it all.

DAR. Have you?

FINBARR. Yes, and if you were around, you'd know.

DAR. Get out. I've work to do.

FINBARR. Get out? You've work to do? No. No, I won't. If you're so dead set on this, then fine. I'll be your next customer. (*Finbarr defiantly loosens his belt.*)

DAR. What? Oh, no. No.

FINBARR. What are you gonna do, discriminate against me? Coupon. You have to honour my coupon now that you've cashed it.

DAR. Surely, I can decline, based on personal matters. (*Finbarr drops his pants.*)

FINBARR. Oh? Declining me, are you? Maybe I'll go straight to your employer's office so? Hmmm? Kick up enough of a stink on the social medias that no one ends up coming here and you lose your job.

DAR. You wouldn't.

FINBARR. Do I look like I'm joking to you? (*The Father and son stare at each other with defiance.*)

DAR. Do you want me to give up, is that it? Just

accept that Mum's gone far too early and just leave it and never try?

FINBARR. She's not gone yet. All this stuff Dar, whatever you're doing here ... it's all wank ... sorry- it's not real. You're gonna have to face the truth. Years down the line, if you don't spend the last days with her, it's gonna be the biggest regret of your life. I'm proud of you, son, we both are ... you can do anything you want ... but you can't reason your way out of this one ... and ... if you don't face it ... it's gonna tear you up from the inside out and I don't want ... I don't want to see what that will do to you in the future.

DAR. I miss her already.

FINBARR. I know ... but you're thinking too far ahead ... she's still alive and she still gives warm hugs, and she misses you in the here and now, but she loves you too much to say anything. Let's go back to her and we can both miss her when the time comes.

DAR. I don't know if I can face it.

FINBARR. No one really can. Believe it or not, I still can't. But I can sit with her face to face ... and if I can do that ... then so can my son. *(Dar hugs his father.)*

FINBARR. Will we go?

DAR. Yeah. Just pull your pants up please, you look ridiculous. *(Finbarr pulls his pants up and they move to exit. Dar looks around the room and collects his phone. He leaves his equipment).*

THE END

D, D & D

D, D & D was first performed at The International Bar, Dublin on July 4th, 2018. The cast was as follows:

Daniel Manuel Pombo
Deirdre Cherley Kane
D Luke Collins
Director Luke Corcoran
Stage Designer & Costume Jennifer Keane

CHARACTERS

DANIEL. Deeply in love with Deirdre. His parents are divorced,
which makes him very apprehensive about his upcoming proposal.

DEIRDRE. Works hard. Plays hard. Loves Daniel but has her own hang-ups on marriage.

D. The character the couple conjure up while undergoing this unorthodox pre-marriage counselling session.

TIME: Ireland, 2018

SCENE: *The stage is set up with a kitchen on the left. There is a table and two chairs. On the right is a backdrop of a forest. In the corner is a chest filled with various teddy bears. There is a toy lightsaber and a toy sword standing up against the back. A grey blanket is thrown untidily in the corner against the back wall. DANIEL is on stage, reading a handwritten note whilst hanging laminated instructions on the wall.*

DANIEL. 'Hang the instructions on the wall in plain sight for both players.' Got it. *(He hangs them up.)* One twenty faced dice? *(He puts it on the table.)* Got it. One character description page? Got it. Pencil. Got it. One bottle of poitin. *(He looks behind him and picks it up. Gives it a shake and sniffs it. He coughs.)* Ok. Phew. A dragon-shaped bong. *(He takes that out from his bag).* Yep. Yeah. Mad stuff. *(He reads.)* 'And finally, one generous bag of cocaine.' Got it. *(He reads.)* 'Your pre-marriage counselling fantasy adventure game is now ready. Good luck on your quest!' Oh. One more thing ... my own precious ingredient. *(He takes out an engagement ring and holds it with reverence. Enter DEIRDRE.)*
DANIEL. Hey! *(He quickly hides the ring in his pocket, and they kiss.)*
DEIRDRE. Hey.
DANIEL. How was your dinner?

DEIRDRE. It was good. Everyone was asking for you. I told them you were a bit stressed lately so you were having a quiet night in … which I can see is clearly the case …

DANIEL. Well. You know me, bit of a party animal.

DEIRDRE. Oh, yes.

DANIEL. No, no, no. Lemme explain.

DEIRDRE. May I? *(She points at the cocaine as he takes her jacket.)*

DANIEL. Yeah, yeah work away. *(She cuts up a line and snorts it.)*

DANIEL. So, my friend, Karl.

DEIRDRE. Not that lunatic.

DANIEL. I know, he's whacky.

DEIRDRE. Walkin' around with a trolley, telling people he's a druid whilst asking them for a coupon for a chicken roll.

DANIEL. Yeah, yeah, but it's still fascinating what he says. Like I think it's really, really good stuff. *(Deirdre offers Daniel a line which politely declines.)* Some of it's a bit mad now I agree, but if he believes in it so much like … you never know …

DEIRDRE. I got the usual off my mother tonight. Deirdre, you and Dan are together a long time now. A long time. A long, long time. Would ye not think of maybe tying the aul knot?

DANIEL. Oh yeah? *(Wrings his hands.)* Did she? Hmm?

DEIRDRE. Yeah. She's like Mrs Doyle but instead of tea, its feckin' marriage. Go on, go on, go on, go on. She loves you, though. *(She looks up to him for a kiss which he gives.)* So, I say, is marriage really that important, Mam? Like, me and Dan are together so much that we're both just not interested in it. It's never come up once. We have a happy relationship, things are fine, why ruin it with marriage?

DANIEL. Yeah. You're right.

DEIRDRE. And do you know what's the worst? We were both born Catholic. Can you be born Catholic? Anyway … *(she does another line.)* That's really good stuff, sweetheart.

DANIEL. Only the best for my honey bun. Actually, your man was doing a discount. One for fifty or two for one hundre-

DEIRDRE. They make you go on a pre-marriage course before you get married. Like, isn't that the most ridiculous, stupid thing you've ever heard in your life? Going on a course-

DANIEL. Some people might call it an adventure.

DEIRDRE. A silly course. To figure out if you're compatible? Or what is it? To show you the dangerous pitfalls of marriage, blah, blah, blah. We've never been on a course and we're perfectly happy together. Right?

DANIEL. Right. Yep. Totally. *(He stealthily tries to take down the instructions off the wall.)*

DEIRDRE. What's that?

DANIEL. Nothing. It's, eh, nothing. Want another line? *(Deirdre stands up and reads.)*

DEIRDRE. A 'pre-marriage counselling fantasy adventure game' *(Long beat before Deirdre bursts out laughing)* Did you get this off the Catholic Church?

DANIEL. No … I got it off …

DEIRDRE. Wait, it's handwritten …

DANIEL/DEIRDRE. Karl the Druid.

DANIEL. Don't laugh Deirdre. I like all the board games.

DEIRDRE. I know.

DANIEL. And, like … I like Karl, I thought I'd help him out, he was saying that we- I mean, I … I needed this and I just wanted to entertain him and …

DEIRDRE. Did you buy him a chicken roll?

DANIEL. Two.

DEIRDRE. You're very good. *(They kiss.)*

DANIEL. I know you're not mad on the whole marriage thing and yeah, what you said earlier, we don't need it, but I just was thinking we could play the game and just for the craic like, you know? And yeah, it's silly, it's written by Karl the Druid, for fuck's sake. Stupid. This is a stupid idea.

DEIRDRE. Go on so.

DANIEL. Go on? Not the Irish go on so, get out of here, you mean,

go on so - 'let's give it a whirl?'

DEIRDRE. Yeah. You had me at fantasy.

DANIEL. Alright! Okay. Awesome! So ... I'll be the dungeon master.

DEIRDRE. Mmm kinky. *(Daniel rushes to the table. Deirdre slowly follows.)*

DANIEL. So ... instructions. Ok. poitín first. *(He pours out the poitín.)*

DEIRDRE. Do you remember what happened last time you had poitín?

DANIEL. No. No. I don't.

DEIRDRE. We couldn't even wash the sheets, we had to bury your boxers out the bac-

DANIEL. Bottoms up. *(He hands her the poitín.)*

DEIRDRE. You're the dungeon master. *(She salutes as she takes the glass out of his hand.)* Isn't this just typical Irish? Get plastered on poitín before a marriage counselling session-

DANIEL. -Adventure.

DEIRDRE. Sure, you'd get on with anyone after this. You'd get up on anyone as well. Get up on a goat, even.

DANIEL. No, no. This is really cool. The idea is to 'get you into an altered state of consciousness-'

DEIRDRE. Oh, I like that!

DANIEL. '-to raise your vibration up to a higher spiritual level. And then to play the game all the way through to its climax.

DEIRDRE. Ooh vibrations and climaxes. I like them too. *(They 'cheers' each other.)*

DANIEL. Slainte.

DEIRDRE. Slainte. *(They drink the poitin. Daniel sputters whilst Deirdre takes it in her stride.)*

DANIEL. 'A generous line'… what's generous? *(Deirdre nods as if to say 'she knows' and cuts them both a generous line. They snort. Similar reactions from both.)*

DEIRDRE. Whooooo! *(Daniel reads the instructions.)*

DANIEL. 'And then the bong'. Ok. This stuff is gonna be mad, alright?

DEIRDRE. Let's do it. *(They both laugh, the effects of both the cocaine and poitin are working on them.)*

DANIEL. Ladies first?

DEIRDRE. Oh, no. I think you should go first on this one, love. *(He nods fearfully. He lights the bong, takes a long inhale and explodes sputtering.)*

DEIRDRE. You're such a lightweight. *(She takes some and sputters too.)*

DEIRDRE. Jesus. What's in that?

DANIEL. It came from-

DEIRDRE. The druid?

DANIEL. The druid.

DEIRDRE. So, what's next?

DANIEL. We write our character.

DEIRDRE. Just the one?

DANIEL. Well, the dice does it. *(He shows the twenty-sided dice and rolls it.)* Ok, gender: male. *(The grey blanket in the corner begins to move and shake.)*

DEIRDRE. Sexist dice.

DANIEL. It's right there. Age? *(She takes the dice and rolls.)*

DEIRDRE. Immortal. *(The grey blanket grows big and shakes a lot, unbeknownst to them both.)* Oh … immortal. Does that mean we'll just win the game?

DANIEL. Let's find out. Class? *(He rolls.)* Dwarf. *(The blanket goes down to a smaller size.)* Ok. Clothes and attire.

DEIRDRE. Naked! *(The blanket falls off, exposing the character of D, standing in a black pair of boxers, facing the crowd with his hands on his hips.)*

DANIEL. Green pants and boots. *(He rolls again whilst D quickly dresses).* And a green shirt.

DEIRDRE. Great. Sounds like we conjured up an immortal fucking leprechaun. *(D throws Deirdre a filthy look.)*

DANIEL. He's not a leprechaun, he's a dwarf. Like Gimli in Lord of the Rings, or Tyrion in Game of Thrones or-

DEIRDRE. Michaeldy Higgins. Mickey-Deee! *(She is highly amused
at her own joke.)*

DANIEL. Weapons.

DEIRDRE. Lightsaber. *(D runs to the corner and flips out the lightsaber, delighted and ready for action.)*

DANIEL. We must let the dice decide, honey. And a lightsaber would just flash through everything and the game would be over too quick, and it would be disappointing for both of us.

DEIRDRE. A bit like you after the poitin.

DANIEL. What? *(She takes the dice and smiles.)*

DEIRDRE. Rolling.

DANIEL. A sword! Cool! What shall we name him?

DEIRDRE. Michaeldy. All one word.

DANIEL. Deirdre, can you please take this seriously?

DEIRDRE. A big bag of cocaine, poitín, whatever's in that bong, I am completely out of me box by the way, an immortal green leprechaun-

DANIEL. Dwarf!

DEIRDRE. Dwarf. And you want me to take this seriously? Fine. Ok. *(She sits down and ruffles his hair.)*

DANIEL. Oh, wait. Karl said that the character's name should have a link between both of us. Ok. Cool. How about instead of Michaeldy ... just, D?

DEIRDRE. D?

DANIEL. D for Dan and D for Deirdre and D for D. *(At this stage, D has changed into another green t-shirt but this one has a giant 'D' printed on it in black. He stands, ready for his quest.)* 'You have now successfully conjured your character from the ether! You are ready to begin your quest'. Great! 'Beware not to break the three rules-'

DEIRDRE. Woo-hoo we're ready! Give us another bit of that poitín will ya?

DANIEL. Yeah. It says take as much as you need. But we need to

be careful of the rule- *(She gulps down a small shot.)*

DEIRDRE. Come on, just get a move on, will ya? I haven't got an eternity! Like little D! *(D shoots her an evil look.)*

DANIEL. Ok. You find yourself at the entrance to a dark and mysterious forest. You look around. *(D acts out all the descriptions.)* It is the 'Foreboding forest of Engagement'. Do you enter-

DEIRDRE. Run.

DANIEL. Away?

DEIRDRE. No, in. If we're in this adventure, we're in this adventure all the way. *(She takes the dice.)*

DANIEL. Ok, but there might be- *(Deirdre has rolled*

and looks
at the result of the roll.)
DEIRDRE. Sprint! *(She claps her hands.)*
DANIEL. Traps. Ok, No. Ok. You sprint into the forest of matrimony *(D sprints on the spot furiously)* but you have sprung a trap, told you, you fall deep, deep, deep- *(D points his finger, as if he has remembered something, and pulls down the forest back drop, revealing a cave/dungeon background.)*
DEIRDRE. Oh, deep? *(D mimes falling from a skyscraper)*
DANIEL. Deep down and find yourself in the 'Dungeon of hastily taken, regrettable decisions'. *(D screams, landing on his back. Dan is looking for a kiss from Deirdre, but she notices D and screams. Dan then notices D and he scream too. They both back up against the wall, away from D.)*
DANIEL. Oh. My. God!
DEIRDRE. Oh my God, oh my God, oh my God.
DANIEL. This. Is. AWESOME! He's just like we described him. Are you seeing him too?
DEIRDRE. There's a fucking leprechaun in our kitchen.
DANIEL. He's a dwarf, but yes, you are seeing him. *(Daniel waves and D waves back.)*
DEIRDRE. Fuck off out of our kitchen, you little leprechaun bastard! *(She marches towards him, but Daniel stops her.)*
DANIEL. No. No. No. No. Karl said whatever you do - do not touch your character - I didn't know what he meant, he's always coming up with these sexual innuendos, but I think he's right. *(Daniel waves again and D smiles and waves back and taps his wrist to say - 'let's get moving'.)* Oh, right, yeah, yeah. Ok. *(He turns to Deirdre.)* Okay, babe. It's alright. You've been through worse or better trips. Let's just play

this out, ok? It's perfectly safe, alright?

DEIRDRE. Ok. Ok. *(She starts laughing.)* There's a fuckin' dwarf in our kitchen.

DANIEL. There is a fuckin' dwarf in our kitchen. *(D clears his throat, making Deirdre jump. D taps his 'watch'. Daniel calms Deirdre down with another line of cocaine).* It's ok. It's ok. *(He smiles and invites her to sit down, she obliges.)* It's grand, he can't hurt you. Will you, D? *(D shrugs).* Alright. Comforting. Okay. *(D gestures for him to hurry up, Daniel rolls the dice.)* You travel deeper into the dungeon, which grows darker and darker. What do you do? Please don't say sprint again.

DEIRDRE. What can we do?

DANIEL. Well, if there's no light in the dungeon, we should …

DEIRDRE. Yes, excellent. We light a torch. *(D takes out a small pink lighter out of his pocket and 'lights a torch'.)*

DANIEL. Excellent, honey, well done. Good move. Thanks D! *(D shakes his head in disgust).* With the massive torch lit, you can now see all the way into the dungeon and in front of you, there is a large red door …

DEIRDRE. Knock it down, D!

DANIEL. Oh, you're really getting into it now! Nice! Ok … *(He
rolls the dice.)* Charge! *(D 'runs' at the door and bursts it open to his amazement. He mimes congratulating the couple, then turns back to where the 'door' is and is aghast. He looks up and up and up …)*

DANIEL. Oh, no!

DEIRDRE. What?!

DANIEL. We've stumbled up on the secret lair of the 'Stationary Squid … Familiarity' and she's just after breeding one of her offspring … 'Contempt!'

A giant evil seal stands before you! *(D readies himself with his sword, realises he has forgotten something, goes to the chest and takes out a seal teddy and places it in front of him. He then gets ready to fight again.)*

DEIRDRE. Oh no!

DANIEL. What?

DEIRDRE. It's huge!!!

DANIEL. I know, it's cool, isn't it?

DEIRDRE. What do we do?

DANIEL. We can run away or … confront the evil beast! *(He offers her the dice which she takes and rolls)*. FIGHT! FIGHT, D!

DEIRDRE. Wooo! Go D! Fight that evil monster. *(D engages in a mighty battle with the teddy seal. It claws at his neck. He drops his sword to defend himself. He holds it away, only to be proven too weak. He manages to punch it in the face a few times but is attacked on the neck again.)*

DEIRDRE. My heart! Daniel, this is so exciting! *(She holds his hand.)*

DANIEL. I'm so glad you like it. You know how much I love making these games.

DEIRDRE. Aww, you put so much effort in.

DANIEL. I wanted you to enjoy it as much as I do.

DEIRDRE. You're so sweet.

DANIEL. So, do you think we're at that higher state of consciousness yet?

DEIRDRE. There's a lepre- dwarf in a vicious battle to the death with an evil sea monster, so yes … I'd say so. Do you know what else is supposed to be reeeally good in an altered state of consciousness …?

DANIEL. More cocaine? *(Deirdre whispers something that surprises Daniel. They kiss passionately. Meanwhile, D has finally got the upper hand on the* *seal. He turns over his sword and clubs it to death. Exhausted, he falls down but stands up again, resolute in his quest. He waits for instruction but sees the pair are too busy kissing to notice him. He waves to no avail. He clears his throat. Nothing. He goes to the lightsaber, picks it up and 'tears' an imaginary door into the kitchen.)*

D. Excuse me? *(He points the lightsaber at the couple which gets their attention.)* I've been in there in a bloody fight to the death with that evil being, on your behalf. I almost lost a limb. And yous are here just mooching away? I don't bloody think so.

DANIEL. Now, now, D, we can get back to the game-

D. Game? Look at that big bloody carcass. *(He picks up the seal teddy.)* That must be twenty feet long. Does this look like a GAME to you pal??

DEIRDRE. No, no, of course not, we're sorry.

D. Not. Yet. You're not. *(He points the lightsaber, which, in their altered state, they believe to be real.)*

DANIEL. Be careful with that thing! It's not a toy!

DEIRDRE. Please D! No!

D. Yes! In! Go on! *(He forces them in through the tear into the 'other side' and 'closes the tear' between the worlds.)*

D. Ooh yes. *(He laughs and does a line himself.)* The good stuff. Whoooo! *(The couple clutch to each other in fear.)* Aw, it's so good to be on the other side for once. You got any of that poi-tin stuff?

DANIEL. Yes, it's right there in front of you, maybe we could do a trade … you can have some if you let us out of here.

DEIRDRE. There's a bong there too, it's really good stuff you can have that too if you let us out.

D. You know what? You're both half right. I 'can' have the poitin and the bong. As for letting you out

… naaah … I wanna see how you handle fighting to the death with evil monsters! *(He drinks the poitin and does the bong.)*

DEIRDRE. Dan, this is a really, really bad trip. Worse than when we went to Mullingar.

D. Ouch.

DANIEL. No. No. There has to be something in the rule book about this … maybe there's a way out through that? *(Points at the rules on the wall.)*

D. What? This rulebook? *(D takes the laminated paper down off the wall, tries to tear it up, but fails.)* What is this foul magic? *(Deirdre laughs triumphantly while Daniel thinks).*

DANIEL. Oh … D? We have a huge, blazing torch here *(he picks up the lighter.)* You can use this to burn the instructions if you change places with us?

D. Ok.

DEIRDRE/ DANIEL. Really?

D. No! You must think I was born yesterday! I'm immortal, remember? Although, technically, today is my birthday.

DEIRDRE. Happy Birthday.

DANIEL. Happy Birthday.

D. And that makes me really sad. *(Starts to cry.)*

DEIRDRE. Oh no … you poor thing … *(Deirdre slinks towards D, who, without looking, points the lightsaber at her.)*

D. But what does cheer me up is one of my favourite past times … emotionally torturing mortals. And taking a fuck load of cocaine! *(He does another line.)* OK! I am your new dungeon master, welcome to *(he reads)* 'pre-marriage counselling fantasy adventure game', who writes this shit, seriously? Okay. I have my characters. Dweeby Daniel and Dopey Deirdre.

DANIEL. Hey!

DEIRDRE. Hey!

DANIEL. If you're gonna play, play nice! *(D shakes his head.)*

D. You walk through the dungeon. The 'stationary squid of familiarity' observes you with a cold gaze, unable to move, she plots her revenge. Her evil offspring vanquished, you're very welcome by the way! You tread forward into ... another dank and ominous corridor ... *(D nods to Daniel and to the backdrop.)*

D. *(Mumbles.)* The backdrop.

DANIEL. What? *(D nods to the backdrop again.)*

D. *(Through gritted teeth.)* The backdrop.

DANIEL. What?

D. The fuckin' backdrop!

DANIEL. Oh. *(He takes down the backdrop at D's behest and reveals the backdrop of a corridor, with torches on either side.)*

D. Actually, gimme that.

DANIEL. The backdrop? *(D shakes his head.)* My fiancée?

DEIRDRE. Fiancée?

D. The damn chest, ye haggis. *(Daniel drags the chest across the stage and gives it to D, who holds him in place with the lightsaber.)*

DEIRDRE. Did you say fiancée? Are you planning a propo-

DANIEL. -Slip of the tongue, darling. Ha. *(D holds the dice and shows it to the couple.)*

D. What would you like to do?

DEIRDRE. Tell me the truth.

D. Rolling for truth. *(He watches the dice.)* Critical hit.

DANIEL. Yes, I'm planning to propose, in fact I've

been planning it for a good few months now. *(He covers his mouth, shocked by what he's just revealed.)*

DEIRDRE. Daniel. No, no, no, get me out of here. If this is some trick into getting you to marry me …

DANIEL. No, it's not a trick. I really didn't wanna say that. It was something I was keeping for myself, just playing around with the idea.

DEIRDRE. Get me out of here!

D. You have dilly-dallied in the corridor for too long. The 'Monster of the White Lie' has come to damage your relationship while you are weak! *(D throws a teddy bear from the chest that lands right in front of the couple. They both scream in terror.)*

D. What would you like to do, adventurers?

DANIEL. Run!

DEIRDRE. Get me fuckin' out of here!

D. Rolling. *(He watches the dice as the couple squirm in fear)*. Fight! Ooooh ho-ho. This is gonna be good.

DANIEL. Deirdre. Get behind me, sweetheart. I'll protect you. *(Daniel grabs the swords and Deirdre gets behind him. Daniel picks up the teddy and engages in a fierce and brutal battle. D shadowboxes as he watches.)*

DEIRDRE. Look out for his claws! *(Daniel screams in pain as the arm of the teddy hits his arm. He pins him against the wall.)*

DANIEL. Roll for damage!

D. Rolling! Ooooh. You have rolled a one. *(Daniel gives the teddy a tiny slap on the nose.)*

D. It is ineffective.

DANIEL. Roll again. *(The teddy bear is getting the better of Daniel.)*

D. Rolling. Shit.

DANIEL. What?

DEIRDRE. What?

D. Critical hit! *(Daniel laughs as he pins the teddy*

against the wall and slits its throat.)
DEIRDRE. Honey, are you ok? *(Daniel is exhausted.)*
DANIEL. I'm … ok. I'm … ok.
DEIRDRE. There's blood all over you. *(Deirdre takes out a napkin and wipes Daniel's face.)*
D. Lucky. You take your relationship and continue the adventure of your pre-marriage quest. Oh ho!!! You've found it! I can't believe you've stumbled upon this. Most couples don't make it this far! The 'Tomb of … your family of origin'! Dun. Dun. Duuuuuun! *(Deirdre has taken up the sword.)* The family of origin is the pinnacle of your quest. Will you, Dopey Deirdre-
DANIEL. Hey!
D. -end up with a man that's just like your father? Will you, Dweeby Daniel-
DEIRDRE. Hey!
D. -end up marrying someone just like your … mother! But first … the 'Woe of financial difficulties' assaults you before you enter the roo- *(D throws another teddy bear in front of Deirdre that she boots full force into the audience.)*
DEIRDRE. No! *(There is a stunned silence from everyone.)*
D. Eh … where did that go?
DANIEL. That was about a hundred feet tall. Deirdre … you're really, really strong.
D. No. She's not. *(He fervently reads the character notes.)*
DEIRDRE. Yes, I am. *(She poses like a superhero.)*
DANIEL. She just kicked a hundred-foot monster into the abyss!
(D holds up Deirdre's stats.)
D. No … it says here, Smelly Deirdre-
DEIRDRE. I thought I was dopey Deirdre?

D. -Has a strength stat of twelve out of one hundred.

DANIEL. How is that possible? (*D flips through the character description.*)

D. Charisma eighty-eight, that's debatable. Speed twenty. Oh ... Oh, ho, ho, ho ... here we go.

DANIEL/DEIRDRE. What? (*D goes to the tray of cocaine and offers it to Deirdre, which she takes. He offers it to Daniel.*)

DANIEL. No, thank you, I'm ... full. (*D shows the character description to Daniel with his other hand. He offers the bong to Deirdre which she accepts.*)

DANIEL. Poison resistance a hundred?

D. Check the next stat.

DEIRDRE. Hooooooo baby. Ok, I'm back in the game!

DANIEL. Addiction one HUNDRED? (*D takes the bong and the cocaine back and puts them on the table.*)

D. Oh yeah ... she's got a mean threshold stat.

DANIEL. Threshold? Is she an addict? Is that why you gave her another line? Is this all 'wearing off' on her? And ... why am I talking to an hallucination?? Deirdre ...

DEIRDRE. Yeah? Come on, let's go! Get behind me, I'll protect you. (*She laughs.*) Whooo. What a game! (*She kisses him on the cheek.*) D, what's the next room?

D. The 'Tomb of the Family of Origin'!

DEIRDRE. Let's go! (*She pulls down the backdrop to reveal a shining white room. D rolls the dice.*)

D. You sprint into the tomb. There is a bright, shining light (*Deirdre and Daniel react, as if blinded.*) Your weapons disappear. (*D snatches the weapons out of the pairs' hands, runs back and sits down.*) You are faced with a six-foot mirror. The 'Mirror ... of

Memory'!

DEIRDRE. Shiny!

DANIEL. Deirdre … I think we need to talk …

DEIRDRE. No, we need to talk to the mirror. Mirror, mirror on the wall, who's the strongest of them all?

D. This isn't a Disney adventure. And the line is, 'who's the fairest of them all?' *(In a squeaky voice)* D … D is the prettiest!

DEIRDRE. Oh my God, it spoke. *(D laughs.)*

DANIEL. No, that was D.

DEIRDRE. Yeah, it said he was the prettiest. Which I wouldn't agree with myself.

DANIEL. Ok. Fuck this game-

D. Fuck you.

DANIEL. -I'm out. D, I need to talk to my fiancée!

DEIRDRE. Fiancée? Are you cheating on me?

DANIEL. No. Not at all. Never in a million years. I love you to

bits.

D. Rolling for truth. Damn. It's true.

DEIRDRE. Awww.

DANIEL. D, can we please stop?

D. You could … if I could tear these rules up but they're protected by some form of indestructible spell. So … you gotta see the game through to its climax. *(He does another line.)*

DEIRDRE. Cliiimaxxx!

DANIEL. Roll for truth!

D. Rolling! Oh, whataya know? True! *(He shows the dice to Daniel.)*

D. Now, get back into the adventure!! *(D whips the lightsaber at him threateningly. Daniel holds his hands up and goes back in.)*

DEIRDRE. Ok, D, what do we do with the mirror? Do we have to fight it?

D. NO!! DO NOT! I REPEAT, DO NOT break that mirror. Untold misfortune will befall those who smashie smashie.

DANIEL. What will happen?

D. Breaking the mirror of memory will drive the breaker ... insane. Mortals cannot handle the memories it will release.

DANIEL. So, what do we do now so I can talk to my fian- partner about what seems, for all intents and purposes, to be an addiction to a class A drug?

D. The two adventurers face the shining mirror of memory. Its brightness glows and then fades ... this is the pinnacle of your 'pre-marriage coun-selling fantasy adventure' ... seriously, whoever wrote this is either taking the piss out of us, or just really, really lazy. TO CONTINUE and be prepared for your imminent marriage, the mirror needs an offering of coin ...

DEIRDRE. Have you any change on you?

DANIEL. No, I used it all on the chicken rolls and ... cocaine.

D. Or jewellery.

DEIRDRE. I hate jewellery. Have you a watch?

DANIEL. I don't think anyone wears watches any-more.

D. Ring. *(D coughs, Daniel shakes his head.)* Engage-ment ring. *(Coughing more angrily.).*

DANIEL. NO!

DEIRDRE. Do you wear rings?

D. OFFER THE ENGAGEMENT RING, YOU CRETIN-OUS FOOL!

DANIEL. Cretinous?

DEIRDRE. Engagement ring? You said this was just a game? For a laugh? You didn't say ... were you going to propose? To me?

DANIEL. No, I ...

D. It was going to propose to me precious, was it ...? *(D crawls across the stage like Gollum)*

DANIEL. Fuck off, D. *(D hisses and crawls back.)*

D. Stupid fat hobbits. *(D does another tremendous line of cocaine in*
character as Gollum.) Tasty, sweet! *(His head falls into the huge pile.)*

DEIRDRE. Daniel? You have an engagement ring.

D. That he should have offered to the mirror aaaages ago. Come oooooooon.

DANIEL. Fine! Fine! Yes *(he takes the engagement ring out of his pocket.)* Yes, I was going to propose because I love you more than anything in the world and marriage might not mean anything to you, but it certainly means a lot to me and if that makes me a 'girly' man or ... a bleedin'... I dunno ...

D. Blouse.

DANIEL. ... a blouse! Then, fine! I'm a big stupid blouse that wants to be married to the love of my life, and I spent thirty percent of my wages on this ...

DEIRDRE. Thirty percent?

DANIEL. ... but it's all for nothing now because I am completely out of my box on cocaine and poitín or whatever, and I'm going to offer it to some imagination mirror-

D. Memory mirror.

DANIEL. -in the middle of my kitchen at the behest of a fucking leprechaun. *(D hisses in defiance, Daniel places the engagement ring down on the floor and stands up.)*

DEIRDRE. Daniel, it's ok.

DANIEL. Oh, yes. Everything's fine. Apart from my failed proposal to a feckin' coke head!

DEIRDRE. What?

DANIEL. Why didn't you tell me?

DEIRDRE. I'm not a coke addict.

D. The mirror has accepted your offering … There is a quick flash of a blinding light. *(The couple react, as if blinded.)*

D. We see a small creature … a skinny, ugly goblin …

DANIEL. That's me. That's me as a kid.

D. Oh. That's a human child? Wow.

DANIEL. Keep going. *(The couple watch, transfixed.)*

D. We see his native domicile. There is a cosy fire lit in the middle of a welcoming house. Goblin child, Daniel, is contently chewing a chocolate bar, his eyes hypnotised by an imagination mirror in the corner.

DEIRDRE. A television. You're watching Lord of the Rings.

DANIEL. No. D. Please, no.

D. A taller female human watches D with a smile in her eyes that quickly turns to sadness. "I'm going away for a while, kid". She kisses him gently on the forehead while he asks "why?". Blackout. We skip to another day. Daniel is on the couch watching a mirror again … he is surrounded by a slimy social worker and his … father. He watches a video he remembers, titled 'your mother still loves you', but he knows it's not true, or else she would be at home with him. Through the video, Daniel learns what heroin is. What other drugs are. Why they're evil and how they took his mother. How she still loves him. Daniel thinks it's his fault. If he were better, she never would have left. He learns when offered to just say-

DEIRDRE. Daniel, it wasn't your f-

DANIEL. No.

D. We skip again to the couch. Daniel sits with the remote control with a hopeful look on his face. He presses the buttons and the mirror springs to life ... but his dad wants to talk. His dad sits down and puts his arm around his son. He smells like tobacco and poitín. "Don't ever get married, son. All you do is open yourself to pain. Pain you can't handle ... promise me, you won't get married". Daniel is scared. His dad is scaring him, so he promises. "Good kid". He gives him a chocolate bar. Daniel doesn't open it. "Don't get married" he repeats ...

DANIEL. Don't get married. *(Daniel has tears in his eyes.)* I just wanted to watch the fellowship of the fucking ring. *(Deirdre takes Daniel's face in her hands. She understands. She picks up the engagement ring and holds it up.)*

D. The mirror accepts Deirdre's offering. There is another flash of light. *(They both react.)*

D. Little goblin Deirdre is in a large, gloomy cavern. There is no cosy fire. It's anything but welcoming but she is on a quest and will not be stalled, not be stopped. In the distance, there is a sleeping, snoring giant on the couch.

DEIRDRE. Shit.

D. She smiles and laughs at the funny snores from the giant. After much effort, she reaches for his large looming leg ... clambers upon him, ready to wake him with a hug, because she knows he likes hugs.

DEIRDRE. Dad.

D. Slowly she climbs, you goblin children are good climbers-

DEIRDRE. Thanks. *(Deirdre watches on with wide eyes.)*

D. -on the giant's belly is a tray with white powdery snow in a lump. She can almost touch his face. Ready to complete her quest, the child stands on the tray to get a foothold and it flips, clanging and clambering to the damp carpet below. The giant awakes! The child smiles until she sees his eyes … the giant, now enraged … she wishes she didn't wake him. He picks her up so fast and before she knows it, she is back where she started her quest, watching the giant move around the cavern like lightening. The giant tries, in vain, to put the powder back in the tray and back into a bag. The giant roars at Deirdre, his breath sending her hair flying back. He loves the powder so much. Even a child can tell if something makes him this angry, it must be because he loved it so much. The child hurt something he loves. The giant loves the powder she thinks … he loves it …

DEIRDRE. … more than me.

DANIEL. Dee …

D. Yes?

DANIEL. Not you! Deirdre … I'm sorry.

DEIRDRE. What have you got to be sorry for? No, you're right, my dad was a coke head. Clearly. That sleeping fucking giant arsehole … and then it's clear in this stupid adventure game or hallucination, whatever this is, that I became a coke head, just like my dad. He gave my mother dogs abuse, and it took fucking ages for her to get him out of our lives … but he kept slinking back and she kept letting him. Borrowing money. Staying over. "I've nowhere else to stay Deirdre". He still borrows money from me when I do hear from him, he's in fucking Thailand trying to start a business. "Just like you, Deirdre, I'm gonna start a business, just like my daughter. My little executive", and we play this game over the phone and we do the usual dance and I give the money and he promises to pay me back, but we both know it's going right up his nose or being pissed up against a palm tree on one of his holidays to Burma. And what do I do? I just ignore it and I, *(D brings over the tray again)* just go off and shove whatever it is up my nose and forget it all. And I try to find whatever care he had for the snow. So, yeah. You're right, I am a coke head. *(She takes a line from D.)* I just don't know how to deal with whatever's inside of me without it. I'm on the bag nearly everyday Dan. Every day. That cannot be healthy. And you want to marry me? You want to marry a coke head? You still want this?

DANIEL. Yes!

DEIRDRE. Even after your dad told you never to get married?

DANIEL. I never wanted to live my life doing what my dad told me to do! In fact, I wanted to do the opposite. Since the first time I met you, I knew you were the woman I was going to spend my life with. My life, Deirdre. That's everything. No one has ever seen that memory of mine. I've never told anyone because … I tried my best to forget about it. And I don't give a shit that you're doing coke, but I am afraid that you're hurting yourself … but it's worse that you're hurting yourself when you don't need to, and you're hurting … without telling me. We can both fix this. We can just put things on hold and focus on healing you. We can work together and get through this … I love you, Deirdre. I love you more than I love adventure games, I love you more than I love Lord of the Rings and … fuck's sake, can't believe I'm saying this … I love you more than your dad loves cocaine.

DEIRDRE. What did you say?

DANIEL. It's insensitive, I know, but it's probably the only way I can get that across to you, in the state you're in right now.

DEIRDRE. Just say it again.

DANIEL. I love you more than your dad loves co-caine.

DEIRDRE. D … roll for truth.

DANIEL. Rolling! Ah, he does love you more than your naughty poppa loves the devil's dandruff! *(Deirdre plants a deep kiss on Daniel's lips and gets down on one knee.)*

DEIRDRE. Dan … *(she holds the engagement ring)* do you want to do what your dad told you never to do?

DANIEL. Are you serious?

DEIRDRE. Daniel … will you marry me?

DANIEL. You're making me the happiest man on the planet. Yes. Yes, I will. *(They hug and kiss again. D watches on with tears in his eyes. He rushes forward and wraps the couple in a hug.)*

EPILOGUE

The couple lovingly stare at each other across the table. D sits in between them, very drunk.

D. True love. Ye just cannae beat it eh? I was in love once. To the beatifulist wee dwarven lassie. She had the fluffiest wee beard. But then, on my one thousand, one hundredth and eleventy first birthday, she left me, for a pointy-eared elvish bastard.

Daniel. We could have rolled an elf?

D. What?

Daniel. Fuck the elves!

D. Aye! *(They clink their glasses)* It's dwarves that go swimming with little hairy women … *(D collapses headfirst onto the table. Deirdre and Daniel hold hands and run off stage.)*

THE END

IMAGINE A MEMORY

Imagine a memory was first performed at The International Bar, Dublin on 4th July 2018.
The cast was as follows:
Sean Conor Hackett
Jack Luke Corcoran
Director Jason Deeney
Stage Designer & Costume Jennifer Keane

CHARACTERS

JACK. A tortured artist. He is constantly looking for that elusive creation of art that will bring him peace. Younger than Sean.

SEAN. A 'coulda been, shoulda been and would've

been'. He regularly falls into fantasies and plays them out in order to escape his current life. Older than Jack.

TUBS. An amalgamation of the voices of 'The Late Late Show' hosts.

JULIE. The voice of Jack's ex-girlfriend and Sean's wife.

TIME. Sometime in Ireland.

SCENE: There is a couch (or armchair) left of stage with an old television set to its right, in an L-shape. There is an easel with a large canvas on it. Underneath the easel, old newspapers are strewn out to catch the paint. There is a six pack of beer between the couch and the TV. There is a coffee table in front with a large remote control on top of it. There is a light box with 'APPLAUSE' written on it. The light is off. The TV comes to life and the 'The Late Late Show' theme song from the 80's plays *(the theme song comes in and out of distortion)*.

TUBS. Ladies and gentlemen, to whom it concerns, it's The Late Late Show. And here is your host, Ryan Tubs. *(The voice of the announcer comes in and out of distortion as the light box turns on.)* Years ago, on a warm summer's night, our first guest of the night had his first comedy gig in his local pub in Dublin and the rest, as they say, is history. Would you please put your hands together, for our first guest, Mister Sean … *(the voice cuts off as the music gets louder and the light box turns on. Sean steps on stage and soaks in the applause. He eggs the audience on for more applause and theatrically puts his hands to his ears. He eventually takes a seat.)* How about that for a welcome, Sean? Does it ever get old?

SEAN. Hate it, yeah. It's really boring, people applauding you for literally walking into a room and sitting on a couch. It's not that difficult, really. You can be as good as me one day too, you know.

TUBS. How does it feel to be back in Dublin after all these years abroad? America, Canada, Australia, the U.K.

SEAN. Feels like I never left. It's just like being at home. *(He gestures to the six pack of beers.)* May I? *(He reacts as if given permission by the TV and cracks open a beer.)* There are so many Irish people over there, it's just like being at home. Except it's far more lucrative. When you're at home, you think Bosco is a sap but then ... it's like, the further away you get from Ireland, the more nationalistic you become. It's as if there's this meter that increases exponentially with distance ... by the time you're across the Atlantic, you're in an Irish pub, drinking Guinness, singing about the rare aul times and doing a 'Michael Flatley' on the tables ... and that's just the stopover to Toronto.

TUBS. It was 25 years ago to the day that you had your comedy debut in your local pub. In your upcoming autobiography, you spill all about that fateful night. Do you care to tell us about it?

SEAN. Oh, I don't think my editor will be too happy with me talking about the contents of my book to such a large audience, and I'm especially not sure about talking about my book to all the people watching live on the internet.

TUBS. Do we want to hear him talk about this chapter in his life? *(The APPLAUSE box lights up. Sean waves them down.)*

SEAN. Let me set the scene. I'm my younger self. I'm a bit of a dope ... *(JACK walks on stage wearing blue dungarees with paint from his art work all over* *them. He carries a paint brush and paint mixer and moves to the easel.)* A bit of a massive dope in my younger years, to be honest. Impulsive. Reckless.

JACK. Talking to Tubs again?

SEAN. Yes, I'm telling him how much of a reckless, irresponsible fool I was when I was younger.

JACK. Says the man drinking a can of cheap piss on imaginary television every night.

SEAN. Do you mind, I'm telling them the story of my first comedy gig. *(He turns back to the TV, smiling.)*

JACK. I do mind because you're not funny. I'm not funny. And I never wanted to be a comedian.

SEAN. Yeah, well, I did.

JACK. But you're not funny.

SEAN. Yeah, well, you can't paint, all your paintings are crap, you once drew a lion with five legs and your teacher laughed at you, remember?

JACK. I was four years old, and that teacher was a wagon.

SEAN. That was funny, wasn't it?

JACK. Howaya Tubs!

TUBS. *(Distorted)* Howaya Jack.

JACK. Don't listen to him, Tubs, he's full of shit and he's not funny. He's not a comedian, he's just a waster, sitting on the couch, acting like he's somebody, but he's a nobody.

SEAN. Don't listen to him, Tubs. Why are you so difficult? I don't disturb you when you're painting, so why do you have to disturb me when I'm on The Late Late Show? This is a big moment for me and you're trying to make it all about you.

TUBS. Gentlemen. The story? *(Sean stands, pleading with Jack.)*

JACK. Yeah sure, go on, yeah. I'd love to hear the story about how I became a man, sitting on a couch, fantasising about being on The Late Late Show, in an imaginary world that doesn't exist. I'll give it to you, thought this might actually be funny … go ahead. Pretend I'm not here. *(Sean continues his painting, its contents are hidden from the audience.)*

SEAN. Wish I feckin' could.

TUBS. Hmm?

JACK. Hmm? *(Sean jumps on the couch, crossing his legs towards the TV.)*

SEAN. I'm here. *(The APPLAUSE box lights up.)* One of the hottest days of the year. I had this planned for months and if there's one thing I love, it's planning. Every minute detail of my life, down to the hour, the minute even. I'm at the bus stop … and I'm the kind of person who would rather be four hours early than one minute late. So … five hours before the show starts, I'm at the bus stop.

JACK. I fucking hate that bus. They shot a gun through the upstairs window that summer.

SEAN. It was a toy gun.

JACK. Metal ball bearings aren't toys. What kind of state do you have to be in mentally, to look at a bus … take up an airsoft rifle, and shoot a ball bearing through the upstairs window.

SEAN. No one was hurt.

JACK. Someone could have been … but no one gave a shit … no Garda investigation, no solution, no suggestions, just … the bus didn't go through that area any more.

SEAN. Fascinating little story, Jack, but I'm in the middle of something here. Maybe you can park that thought? *(Turns to TV.)* So, I'm at the bus stop, and I get a text from Julie.

TUBS. Your wife

JACK. Your wife?? You married her??

SEAN. Yes. My wife! Not at the time, she wasn't. The kind of text that makes your heart sink, right down to your butthole. "We need to talk". When you get that-

JACK. I'm sorry. You married Julie?

SEAN. I've been stuck with you for days, and this is my time now. If you don't respect that I'm going to tell them about the time you waddled into first class with your pants around your ankles, asking the teacher to wipe your bum.

JACK. *(Beat.)* It happened to you too.

SEAN. Yeah, well, I'm mature. *(Jack is exasperated but concedes. Sean turns to the TV.)* I had five hours. Why not, ya know? I got the bus in the opposite direction, hopped the fence, and she let me in. She tells me she cheated on me when she was on holidays. Now, this was the biggest day of my life. The comedy gig. And she tells me when she was on holidays with her mum in Ibiza, she shifted a guy called Mickey.

JACK. What an appropriate name.

SEAN. I'm there for hours, she's crying, my hearts broken at this stage, but I just say … this is the one thing I'll concede to my younger self … he had a real skill and propensity for just saying 'fuck it' to everything. Do a comedy gig? Fuck it, let's go. Drop out of college? Fuck it.

JACK. Just walk straight out of your cheating girl's house, without saying anything?

SEAN/JACK. Fuck it.

SEAN. I'm at the bus stop. Forty-eight minutes to spare. Bus'll be along in eight. It's not too bad, I'll be a couple minutes late. I'm frantic, sweating in my suit, my mind and stomach reeling. I'm going over my notes and jokes and all I hear is "sorry pal, you got a smoke?" and before I can say 'I don't smoke' …

BANG ... I see flashes of an explosion out the side of my eyes, and I go down. All I see is black. And I wake up, no phone, no wallet, just quickly cooling blood on my head and all over my cards. So, I sit up, I just know I have to get to the gig. As I sat up, wouldn't you know, the bus stops and I take it as a sign. Bus driver - "You alright?" I hop on. "Drive", I say. "Drive".

TUBS. We interrupt this programme to bring you a special bulletin. *(Jack finds this hilarious.)*

JACK. Your imaginary Late Late Show is so boring, it's being interrupted.

TUBS. Ladies and gentlemen, to whom it may concern, let me introduce our next guest ...

JACK. Even better, you've been replaced!!

TUBS. *(Distorted.)* Julie.

SEAN. Julie? Julie, I'm here! I'm here!

JACK. Her?

JULIE. Hi, sweetheart. You're nice and warm. I've been looking up online about this ... if you can hear me ... lots of people say you can, and I should keep talking.

JACK. No. No. No.

JULIE. I don't know what to say, you're the one who's always good at talking. Why can't we have nice things happen to us? Hmmm? Why can't we? *(Julie cries.)* It's not fair. Wake up! Wake up!

SEAN. I'm awake!! Julie!! *(The Late Late Show theme tune starts playing again, distorted.)*

SEAN. Why can't she hear me?

JACK. *(Long beat as Jack leans over his canvas.)* Because we're in a fucking coma. I'm in a fucking coma ... but I don't get it, I broke up with her.

SEAN. Why would you break up with her?

JACK. Cheating! It's the one thing that no relationship can recover from. It's just dead after that. Like ripping everything away, and all that's left, is a void. No one deserves to be forgiven for that and people like that are just constantly self-destructive. And are you telling me, you forgave her?

SEAN. Obviously, if she's outside waiting for us. Me! Waiting for me!

JACK. None of this makes sense. Fuck. Which one of us owns this body?

SEAN. What do you mean?

JACK. You can remember. My five-legged lion and shitting my pants in school … and the bus stop. Julie cheating. But I can't remember any of your crap.

SEAN. What crap?

JACK. Sold-out comedy gigs? Late Late Show? Toronto?

SEAN. That's not crap, that happened.

JACK. No, it's a fantasy. Fantasy is make-believe, so you're just make-believe. HEY! GET ME OUT OF HERE! I'M THE REAL ONE!

SEAN. Oh yeah? What happened after I got on the bus?

JACK. Oh, come on. I just broke up with my cheating girlfriend and I got mugged. It's always been sketchy, and you know that.

SEAN. Yeah, but I know exactly what happened, and so do you.

JACK. You've no proof. *(Sean presses the remote control, we hear a bus start-up and drive. They both watch the memory on the TV.)* Yeah, OK. I put the tie from the suit around my head to stop the bleeding.

SEAN. There was a lot of blood on your- our head.

JACK. Wait … did we pay?

SEAN. What?

JACK. The bus fare?

SEAN. Oh. No. Bus driver was terrified, look at him.

(They both laugh. We hear the bus come to a halt and open its doors.)

SEAN/JACK. Thank you.

SEAN. At least you remembered to thank him. *(We hear running and heavy breathing.)*

JACK. Fast forward.

SEAN. But you're gonna miss jumping over the dog, it was great, I have a cool camera angle from underneath, looking up. *(Jack looks at Sean and he fast forwards.)*

SEAN. OK, here. The main guy is just finished, he's walking off and yeah, there you are, getting the announcer's attention, and there you are. Star swipe. Do you like that editing? Enter young Sean, doing his material to a raucous crowd.

JACK. That never went viral though.

SEAN. Oh, it did, after a few years. It was buried on some local server. I did a whole skit based on it. People didn't believe it, so they found the video and it went viral. Career *(he makes an airplane noise)* boom.

JACK. No. This is … you're not funny.

SEAN. I beg to differ.

JACK. Tell me a joke.

SEAN. I'm not a performing monkey.

JACK. I beg to differ.

SEAN. OK. What does a Dublin owl say? 'Who'. Or a Dublin jack
russell? 'Righ righ righ'. Or an inner-city cat? 'Noooooo'.

JACK. You toured the whole Irish diaspora with those 'funny jokes'. My sides are killing me. OK. What other unbelievably ridiculous choices am I supposed to have made with my life.

SEAN. It's my life too, first of all, and they weren't ridiculous.

JACK. You got back with Julie.

SEAN. Oh, I did more than get back with her, kid ...

JACK. I don't need to know the details.

SEAN. Oh yes, you do. Married. *(Sean shows the ring on his finger.)*

JACK. Aww you fucking idiot. *(Jack sits down on the couch, deflated.)*

SEAN. I know you are, but what am I?

JACK. I wanted to break up with her for years. I just never had the courage.

SEAN. Oh yeah, really brave thing, breaking a poor girl's heart.

JACK. And what about mine? She did it once, she was probably cheating on me the whole time. I had no one to talk to about it, sure Ma and Da were useless at all this stuff.

SEAN. 'Don't mind them'.

JACK. Yeah. 'Don't mind them'. I always wondered how Ma would get on, working for an emergency phone line. "Howaya, the landlord's gonna kick me out, I don't know what to do?" "Don't mind them, love". "Listen, the welfare's after cutting my dole off". "Don't mind them".

SEAN. Yeah. "Eh, listen, I'm after taking a load of these pills and- *(the distorted theme song plays.)*

TUBS. *(Distorted)* Your next guest, Julie.

JULIE. Hey. I'm back again. Your ma left flowers, they're beautiful, look at them. I got your magazines. I know you love your video editing; you can catch up on them when ... your ma's around nearly every day now. She's a strong woman, your mother. I told her the nurses were annoying me, trying to rush me out after hours. "Don't mind them" she said. So, I didn't. I needed to tell you anyway. I don't know how long I can keep this up. I'd be here forever, I would, I promise you ...

JACK. She's leaving?

SEAN. Ssshhh!

JULIE. We just ... those flowers smell gorgeous ... we might not be able to afford it. And I'd hate to have to just give up ... not even to give up ... to be forced to give up over something as stupid as money. But that's the reality. So, if you plan on waking up, can you do it soon please? Real soon? I miss you so much. Look at the flowers, just look at them ... even just smell them please, will you ... *(distortion.)*

SEAN. JULIE! I CAN SEE THEM! I CAN SEE THEM! They're wonderful ... they smell gorgeous, you're right ...

JACK. This is fucked man.

SEAN. She's right there, why can't she hear me?

JACK. No ... she said she was back ... that my ma visited ... she got flowers ... all that happened, and that was only two minutes since her last message ...

SEAN. What do you mean?

JACK. I mean, we must be in this coma for ages. Days? Weeks? Oh God. What if I wake up inside your body?

SEAN. I'm all for experimentation but that's a bit much, even for me.

JACK. Not funny! What if I wake up and I've aged like ... this ... and that is my life? This is a nightmare.

SEAN. What's so bad about being me, huh? What's so bad about my life? What would you do? What would you have done?

JACK. I wouldn't have become the world's most unfunny comedian. I would have ...

SEAN. What?

JACK. Painted. I would have painted. Dedicated

myself to my craft and just express myself.

SEAN. In order to become famous for painting.

JACK. No.

SEAN. Yes. Yes, you would have. You didn't care what you did when you were younger, you just wanted to be noticed. To have fame!

JACK. Says the man fantasising about talking to Tubs.

SEAN. Yeah. And I am you, remember? The apple doesn't fall very far from the … apple. Comedy. Video editing … all your hobbies, and not one pursued to its potential. You even wrote a play once with the idea of 'becoming the best playwright in Dublin'. It was crap … and it wasn't even that it was crap, you just didn't have the balls to go out and do it. Take the chance of making a fool out of yourself, so what?

JACK. I like painting because I like painting. *(He goes back to painting.)*

SEAN. What are you doing there? Painting a picture?

JACK. You are wasting your detective skills, going up on that stage.

SEAN. A picture only exists so people can look at it. *(Sean goes to look at the painting.)*

JACK. Get … back … *(Jack threatens him with the paint brush.)*

SEAN. What are you painting?

JACK. None of your business.

SEAN. How are you gonna be an artist if you keep everything to yourself?

JACK. Oh, and comedy is art, is it? 'WHO?' 'Nooooo?' Yeah … gives me goosebumps.

SEAN. Let me see.

JACK. No.

SEAN. Come on.

JACK. Leave me alone.

SEAN. Leave you alone? If you haven't figured it out by now, you are alone.

JACK. Good.

SEAN. That's what you want, isn't it? To be left alone. You want to be artistic, painting away … but you never had the courage to actually show it to the world. Whatever you're making.

JACK. I had the courage to do your viral video, didn't I?

SEAN. That's because you were close to death. Running on pure adrenaline. You were a bit out of your mind … and that makes sense. Maybe that's when I was born.

JACK. Sure.

SEAN. We couldn't be more different. Maybe when you nearly died from that blow to the head, that's where I came in. I took over. That's why you can't remember. Maybe I'm supposed to remember you and … OK … I got it … *(Sean moves towards Jack, going to hug him.)*

JACK. No. Go away.

SEAN. Ssshhh. Ssshhh. I'm supposed to embrace you so I can get out of here.

JACK. No way.

SEAN. This is how these things work, haven't you seen 'Fight Club'? We're the same person. We're both representations of different stages in our life … and I need to embrace you, in order for you to 'move on'.

JACK. Me, move on? No, no, no. I'm the real owner of this body.

SEAN. If you are, then why would you be scared of a little hug?

JACK. I am, but I would never marry Julie.

SEAN. So, then it's fine … this is all fake … nothing

to worry about. Just c'mere … c'mon … (*Sean hugs Jack in an extremely awkward embrace.*)

SEAN. Ssshhh. I remember you. I remember how angry you were. It's OK. It's OK. Jack … young Sean … it's not your fault. It's not your fault.

JACK. You think a line from 'Good Will Hunting' is going to fix all this?

SEAN. It's not your fault. I understand your anger. It's OK. Everything's OK.

JACK. 'Fuck off me. (*He struggles to free himself from Sean's hug.*)

SEAN. Just one more minute.

JACK. No. It's not working. (*He breaks away from the strong embrace.*)

SEAN. You didn't even try.

JACK. What is it, exactly, I'm supposed to try? Crying?

SEAN. Maybe opening up your heart a little bit?

JACK. Opening up my heart? God. I don't think you grasp the seriousness of the situation. We are in a comatose body, (*he points up*) how did we get there, huh? What happened to us? To me?

SEAN. It doesn't matter how we got here; we need to get out. Times running out, like you said, I want to get out of here before Julie sends us another message. They could turn off whatever machine it is keeping us alive. They could pull the plug.

JACK. Maybe they should.

SEAN. What?

JACK. I could be left here, just with my painting. I'd be left alone apart from you. You could have the TV Monday, Wednesday and Friday, and between then, it's peace and quiet.

SEAN. You'd be willing to kill us so you could just paint? No. No way. (*Sean moves to the painting.*)

JACK. Leave it. (*Picks it up and turns it around, to re-*

veal a goldfish in space.)
SEAN. A goldfish?
JACK. It's a 'Space Goldfish'.
SEAN. Clearly. We never had a pet goldfish.
JACK. It's symbolic.
SEAN. So, you'd rather die and be left all your life with a symbol, then get out there and live?
JACK. At least it's authentic.
SEAN. So is this. *(Sean puts his knee up on the couch and lifts the canvas over his head, threatening to break it.)*
JACK. No! *(Jack quickly runs to the remote control and stands in the same pose as Sean.)*
SEAN. That's our only hope of contacting the outside world.
JACK. Put the goldfish down and I'll put the remote down.
SEAN. Fine … on three …
JACK. Fine. Three.
SEAN. Two. *(Long beat.)*
JACK. One. *(Both lower their objects.)*
SEAN. Tell me what it symbolises.
JACK. 'Sake.
SEAN. Tell me what it symbolises, or it's gone.
JACK. It's none of your business.
SEAN. It's as much my business as it is yours.
JACK. I'll smash it *(to the remote).*
SEAN. I'll smash this *(to the canvas).*
JACK. *(Long beat.)* A goldfish will grow exponentially, depending on its surroundings, and if a goldfish could survive in space, then-
SEAN. -then there's no telling how big it could grow. That's actually pretty clever. Now there. Was that so hard, opening up?
JACK. It's not the same, being threatened to open up.

SEAN. *(Long beat.)* Would you like another hug?

TUBS. *(Distorted.)* Julie. *(Sean rushes back to the couch, snatches the remote from Jack and increases the volume.)*

JULIE. Your hand is so warm. How can it be warm still? They said you didn't respond to the treatment ... I didn't understand what they meant ... they lowered your dosage, and you haven't moved ... you haven't even blinked or smiled or ... I don't know what to do. I can't believe this, we can't afford ... Your parents don't know what to do ... the doctors think ... but how can his hand be warm? Tell me how his hand can still be warm?

SEAN. Julie?!

JACK. *(Stunned.)* That's it. We're done. *(Sean is distraught, Jack is stunned.)*

TUBS. We interrupt this programme for a special announcement. *(We hear the distorted theme song. A message from Jack plays through the TV.)*

JACK. O/S. Mam, Dad ... Julie ... I'm sorry. I just can't keep going. I just feel empty all the time, I have for years ... I can't explain it. It's just this empty feeling. Everything tastes like grey ash ... everything sounds like it's underwater and ... I'm sorry. I do love you. I think I do. This isn't your fault. I just can't feel anything anymore. *(There is a sound of pills rattling. Sean looks to Jack.)*

JACK. It's better this way. Just get it over with. *(Distorted noises come from the TV as Julie's voice comes through.)*

JULIE. Please Jack. Just come back. I forgave you for cheating on me. I can forgive you for this if you wake up and promise never to do something so stupid again. I love you so much, you feckin' eejit. If you only knew how much love there was for you ... you'd never have-

SEAN. It's you. She said 'Jack'. You cheated on ... you tried to ...

JACK. How can I go back after what I did to them? *(Jack has sunk to his knees.)*

SEAN. *(Long beat.)* After what you did to yourself, you mean ... I get it, kid ... I get it.

JACK. Do you?

SEAN. I remember it all. You're in a lot of pain, kid ... and the pain is so big, you felt it was too much to bear ... and you're right, it is ... that's what other people are for. You can't keep it to yourself. You have Julie ...

JACK. I fucked that up.

SEAN. And she forgave you. I remember. I remember. You felt so empty inside that you didn't believe she really loved you. If she really loved you, then you could have a one-night stand and she should be able to forgive you ... it was like a test. You don't have to test people, Jack. You can trust people, you know ... I stopped testing people years ago.

JACK. You're not real. *(Sean puts his arm around Jack.)*

SEAN. You can feel me, can't you?

TUBS. Time is running out, ladies and gentlemen. For our last performance, I'd like to introduce ... *(A distorted live performance of music starts playing.)*

SEAN. Stand up. I know you feel empty inside. I know you do. But there is such a thing like a light that doesn't go out.

JACK. Like what?

SEAN. The red light on the TV, for one ... as long as you don't plug it out. Come on, Jack, you gotta fight now!

JACK. I don't know-

SEAN. If you're not gonna fight for you, then fight for me ...

JACK. I just feel empty all the time.

SEAN. Like space? Like space, yeah, but deep down inside of you, there's a goldfish that needs to grow but you're keeping him in a tiny box. That woman there loves you and she's still with you, holding your hand through all of this. You're gonna get back in there, and open up that box, and nurture that fucking goldfish, and show it to the world, and let it grow and grow until it fills up the entirety of that void … and you're going to trust that people love you. Like Julie. Like Mum. Like Dad. Like me.

JACK. But you're not real.

SEAN. No. I'm you. You're dynamite, kid. That painting. Most authentic thing you've ever created. Get back out there.

JACK. What about you? *(Sean picks up the remote.)*

SEAN. I'll be fine. I can reminisce with Tubs about how proud I am of how brave and courageous I was as a younger man … because I opened up.

JACK. Thank you. *(They hug.)*

SEAN. Maybe you can check in every once in a while.

TUBS. Ladies and gentlemen, that's all we have for tonight. I'd like to thank … *(distorted, Jack looks up and shouts.)*

JACK. Julie!

SEAN. Give my love to Julie. *(Jack nods.)*

JACK. Julie. I'm here. I'm here.

JULIE. He's opening his eyes. He's opening his eyes. Nurse!?! Nurse! *(The lights go down and up. Jack has left the stage; Sean is left alone.)*

SEAN. I'm proud of you, kid. I'm proud of you. *(The APPLAUSE box lights up and the distorted theme song starts playing.)*

THE END

HIDDEN; HOMELESS

CHARACTERS

JOSEPH. 45, a large, bull of a man. Sleeping rough for the last five years. Everything about Joseph has hardened, except his heart. A skilled carpenter by trade, with some mental health issues. Years ago, a perfect storm of circumstance forced Joseph to move off his farm. His many friends would describe him as 'salt of the earth'.

MARIAN. 25, Marian works at Sunshine ABC Bank. Long hours at a high-pressure job and burning the candle at both ends has taken its toll on her optimism. Coming home to find she has been evicted, she has no family in Dublin and is forced to spend a night on the street. Her work colleagues would describe her as driven and professional.

TIME: Ireland 2019.
SCENE: *A rainy night in Dublin, outside the Arnotts Christmas window, under the eaves. A colourful sleeping bag has a sleeping occupant, JOSEPH, inside it. He is lying on his side, with his back to the audience. Enter MARIAN, hair wet, in a suit with a sleeping bag and sports bag in hand. She looks around, sees Joseph, asleep in his sleeping bag. She opens her bag, takes out cardboard and sits on it. She wraps the sleeping bag around herself. She takes out a bottle of cheap vodka and drinks. She cries. Joseph, still with his eyes closed, opens his mouth.*

JOSEPH. Cheer up. *(Marian looks straight ahead.)*
MARIAN. Fuck off. *(She swallows her tears and takes a swig of the vodka.)*
JOSEPH. That's nice. Well, if ye need to talk, I'll be here all night. *(He turns around on his other side, still with his eyes closed.)*
MARIAN. I'm sorry. *(Long beat.)* Can I use your phone? *(Joseph sits up.)*
JOSEPH. Do I look like someone who has a phone? Sleepin' bag. Big beard. White hair. Trying to kip outside the fanciest shopping window in Dublin? Do you think I could afford one of those fancy phones?
MARIAN. No. Sorry. *(She puts her head in her hands.)* Jesus Christ.
JOSEPH. No, no. I'm not him. I'm someone better. *(He pulls the sleeping bag over his head and ruffles around a bit. He comes back out with a Santa hat on his head.)*
JOSEPH. Ho! Ho! Ho! Hello, little girl. I see you've been a very good girl this year! What would you like for Christmas? You can have anything you like!

MARIAN. A place of my own.

JOSEPH. Ho, ho, ho. In Dublin? I'm Santa Claus, not a fucking miracle worker. Anything else?

MARIAN. A phone.

JOSEPH. Ho, Ho, *(reaches into the bag)* Ho, Ho Ho. It's somewhere around here. Ha! *(He takes out a mobile phone.)*

MARIAN. I thought you didn't have one.

JOSEPH. Everyone has one these days. Cheap as chips. If you're ringing the centre, don't bother, they won't answer. *(He holds out the phone, Marian stands up to reach it, Joseph takes it back.)*

JOSEPH. What happened your last phone?

MARIAN. It's broken.

JOSEPH. Who broke it?

MARIAN. Look, it's been a really rough day-

JOSEPH. Try a few years.

MARIAN. Yeah, okay, but I really just need to use your phone.

JOSEPH. Who broke it?

MARIAN. I fuckin' smashed it, alright.

JOSEPH. Good for you girl! Good for you! *(He stands up, wearing his Santa hat.)* Fuckin' brainwashing ye these things are. We're murdered out here, murder, that's what this is. No home, no future. Can't even plan tomorrow, that's what it takes away from you. Your life is a cage with a very small window. If that's not a type of murder, I don't know what is ... and this? This *(looks at the phone)* is just a weapon of mass distraction from all the shit going on. *(He goes to smash the phone.)*

MARIAN. Wait, wait, wait!

JOSEPH. What?

MARIAN. I need it.

JOSEPH. Spoken like a true addict. *(He lobs the phone in the air and Marian catches it, much to her* *relief.)*

MARIAN. I'll just be a minute.

JOSEPH. You're not gonna run off with it, are ye? I'm not in the mood for a chase, the aul ligament damage, you know.

MARIAN. Do I look like someone who's gonna steal your phone?

JOSEPH. Have you any spare change? *(Long beat.)*

MARIAN. Do I look like I have any spare change too?

JOSEPH. Yes, on both counts.

MARIAN. You probably have more money than I do right now.

JOSEPH. Are you working?

MARIAN. What does that mean? Like, am I a prostitute?

JOSEPH. I have twenty euro on me right now. In change. In me bag.

MARIAN. Oh God.

JOSEPH. So, you might not have any money right now, but this is all I'll have 'til Thursday.

MARIAN. I'm not a prostitute.

JOSEPH. You've a full-time job.

MARIAN. Yes.

JOSEPH. But you've no money now, I've about twenty euro, so, not right now, but you do have more money than me, in the long term. See?

MARIAN. I thought you were asking if I was a prostitute. *(Long beat.)*

JOSEPH. Well, ye kinda are. It's the same thing, isn't it? Selling your physical body for a nine-to-five, while someone makes a profit from you?

MARIAN. I'm going to make a phone call now, okay? *(Marian takes out the phone and tries to turn it on. Joseph starts singing. She stands up and walks towards Joseph, looking at the phone.)*

JOSEPH. *(Singing)* Should auld acquaintance be forgot, and never brought to mind. Should auld acquaintance be forgot and days of auld lang sy-

MARIAN. What's your pin?

JOSEPH. I thought you were gonna join in for a second.

MARIAN. I really need the pin number …

JOSEPH. Joseph. Friends call me Joe. Big Joe. Little Joe if they're being ironic. Happy Joe. Joseph and his amazing technicolour sleeping bag-

MARIAN. Joseph, can you please tell me your pin number?

JOSEPH. I'd love to …?

MARIAN. Marian.

JOSEPH. And what do your friends call you?

MARIAN. Marian.

JOSEPH. No ironic nicknames? Maid Marian? Cheery Marian? Oh, she of the gloriously joyful disposition?

MARIAN. Pin please?

JOSEPH. Zero, Zero, Zero, Zero. *(Long beat.)* Don't blame me, it came with that vicious piece of machinery. *(Marian types the pin in and makes a phone call, remembering a contact from memory.)* All zeroes, that's what they think of all homeless in this Country. Go to work. Grovel and get a job for a boss. Doesn't matter if your boss is an abuser. No. Just fucking work. Do what you're told. Do what you're told by some abusive animal … until you die … because you're a one and you're making us rich. Or fuck off and die sooner if you're a zero and costing us money. *(Marian is frustrated with her efforts and gives Joseph back the phone.)*

MARIAN. You've no credit. *(She sits back down on her cardboard.)*

JOSEPH. Story of me life. *(Marian starts to cry*

again.) Ah look. Jaysus. I'll get you some, alright? I need to make a few phone calls meself, like.

MARIAN. No, it's okay.

JOSEPH. No honestly, it's fine. Are you homeless, are you?

MARIAN. I've no place to go.

JOSEPH. Where do you live?

MARIAN. I had an apartment in Dublin 2 for years, but they upped the rent. I tried paying it. I did. Fucking sixty-five percent of my wages? No savings. No nest egg. Forget about gettin' a fucking mortgage … or a fella, and the landlord upped the rent before the caps came in.

JOSEPH. Cheeky bollixes. How much were ye payin'?

MARIAN. Fifteen hundred.

JOSEPH. Fifteen hundred? Holy Jaysus. Fifteen grand for rentin' an apartment? I knew it was bad, didn't know it went up that much.

MARIAN. One thousand five hundred, Joe.

JOSEPH. No, I'm talking about per year. That's more than 15. That's 18,000 you gave them, a year. That's a living wage, supposably by this poxy Dail's calculations. You're paying your landlord a living wage? To live? And your company's not paying you enough. Within two years, you could have bought your own plot of land and given the two fingers to your wanker of a boss, who, I presume, is a wanker.

MARIAN. Not everyone is a wanker.

JOSEPH. True enough. But your boss is, isn't he?

MARIAN. Yes.

JOSEPH. Thought so, and your landlord is one by default anyway.

MARIAN. Well, it wasn't all her fault.

JOSEPH. No? Do you wanna scarf by the way? I have a big one here somewhere. Go on, tell us. Tell us while I get this. *(Joseph looks through his rucksack and sleeping bag.)*

MARIAN. I moved in with this fella a few months ago.

JOSEPH. And it wasn't immediate marital bliss? Shocker.

MARIAN. It was actually.

JOSEPH. Well, that's more shockin' to hear than … hang on a second. Did you send a 'call me'?

MARIAN. To who?

JOSEPH. To whoever you were tryin' to ring? You know you can send 'call me's'? They're great. You just pop in the number and they get a message to call you back? Here. *(He wraps the scarf around her and gives her the phone.)*

JOSEPH. It's zero zero-

MARIAN. -Zero zero. Thanks.

JOSEPH. Yeah, go to new message. That's it, hang on. *(He takes the phone, but he can't read it. He looks in his rucksack again.)*

JOSEPH. Tell us anyway, go on, you moved into marital bliss?

MARIAN. Yeah, and it was his place, like. I was delighted we could split the rent and afford it. *(Joseph takes out his reading glasses and puts them on. He taps a few times on his phone.)*

JOSEPH. There ye go, all set up there. Just put the number in. So, you were payin' him. Every month. *(She types in the number.)*

MARIAN. Every month, into his bank account, and he'd pay the landlord … except one day, I came back and I found an eviction letter. *(She presses send on the phone.)*

JOSEPH. Coz he wasn't payin' the rent, he was pocketing the money. *(Joseph laughs at figuring this out).*

MARIAN. No. Well, yeah.

JOSEPH. Ah no, I'm not laughin' at you, just laughin' that I figured it out. I hear a lot of things out here, ye know. I was only sayin' to meself the other night, I have a lot of conversations with meself, ye see. Joseph, I says. Yes, Joseph? Isn't it mad, Joseph, that a lot of people's stories are so different to yours, but on one level, they're so similar? You're right there, Joseph, ye clever bastard. There but for the Grace of God, go I, says Joseph. Says I, we've already been there.

MARIAN. Yeah. We're all only two missed paycheques away from eviction. *(She drinks.)* Except Google.

JOSEPH. And Facebook. *(She drinks again. Joseph puts his hand out for the bottle, she considers giving it to him and after another swig, does so.)*

MARIAN. And Facebook. *(Joseph takes a swig from the vodka.)*

JOSEPH. Grey Goose? Fuck me. Are you sure you're not a millionaire? Is this a hidden camera show? It's lovely, Marian. Thank you. A great way to finish off the year.

MARIAN. Yeah. *(Joseph hands the bottle back.)*

JOSEPH. This your first time out on the streets?

MARIAN. Yeah. *(She gives him the bottle; he takes another swig.)*

JOSEPH. Sláinte.

MARIAN. Cheers. *(She takes the bottle back.)*

JOSEPH. So, what did he say when you showed him the letter?

MARIAN. He … he wasn't happy.

JOSEPH. Well, neither were you, considering you were paying all that money every month.

MARIAN. Yeah, he wasn't happy.

JOSEPH. What's his name?

MARIAN. What's it matter?

JOSEPH. I'd just like to know.

MARIAN. Derek.

JOSEPH. Derek. *(Long beat.)* Does Derek like hitting women?

MARIAN. What?

JOSEPH. He hit ye, didn't he?

MARIAN. No.

JOSEPH. There's no need to keep anything from me, ye know. No secrets on the streets. Only the big open secret of homelessness that everybody puts in the back of their mind … 'til it happens to them. *(Beat.)* Did he hit ye? You can tell me. It doesn't make you weak, ye know. *(She casts her eyes down. Her silence gives Joseph his answer.)*

JOSEPH. Not the first time he did it either, no?

MARIAN. No. *(Suddenly we hear a Nokia 3310 ringtone. Joseph grabs the phone out of Marian's hand and answers.)*

JOSEPH. See you Derek, you fuckin' woman-beating scrawny piece of shit!! *(Marian jumps up to try and stop him.)* You like hitting women, do ye? Well, wait 'til I get a hold of you. I'm gonna break every little bone in your body, you fuckin' coward. Your time is coming, you skinny little fucker. And Happy New Year, ye cunt! *(He screams into the phone. Marian can't believe he's done that.)*

MARIAN. Do you know what you've done to me?

JOSEPH. I didn't do anything, only deal with an open secret. That's how you do it. You confront it. What were you gonna do? Stay with him? Pretend that he didn't rob ye? Pretend he didn't hit ye?

MARIAN. You had no right.

JOSEPH. It's my phone.

MARIAN. I've nowhere to stay now.

JOSEPH. Welcome to my world.

MARIAN. Oh, because you're in the shit, I *should* be in the shit? Because you've nowhere to stay, I *should* have nowhere to stay?

JOSEPH. Not should. *Could*!

MARIAN. Well, I'm here now, Joseph! Here but for the Grace of God, am I. The only person that I know in Dublin I could stay with just got abused over the phone, and he'll blame it on me.

JOSEPH. Abused over the phone? *He* got abused? Jesus, girl, come on. I'll help ye. I'll help ye get another place, alright?

MARIAN. I'm not your property or your responsibility, pal. That was my only hope. *(She sits down again and drinks.)*

JOSEPH. That was before you met Joseph and his amazing technicolour sleeping bag! There has to be someone else you can ring.

MARIAN. I don't want your fuckin' phone, alright? And even if I did, you've no credit, and you're probably going to take the phone back off me again and abuse them.

JOSEPH. *(Shouting and pointing at her.)* Stop sayin' that! I'm not an abuser!! *(Realises his outburst of anger.)* I'm sorry.

MARIAN. I'm gonna find somewhere else.

JOSEPH. Ah, it's dangerous out here.

MARIAN. It's dangerous here. *(She starts gathering up her stuff.)*

JOSEPH. It's not. Well, it is. You remind me of me sister. She loved lookin' after people. Looked after me. Basically raised meself and the brothers … and herself. She was a nurse. I'd see her every week. Then she got with this fella. Soon I'd see her only once a month, every three months, once a year because she knew … if I had seen her with a busted lip, she'd know what I'd do to her fella. Derek his name was. No word of a lie. Little scrawny shit.

MARIAN. -and what did you do to this Derek?

JOSEPH. Nothin'. Coz she asked me not to. I sat there at Christmas dinner one year. Kept the peace. Said nothin'. *(Long beat.)* I just couldn't sit there at the dinner and pretend everything was hunky dory. Biggest regret of me life, not doing anything. Sit down, come on, sit down, you're safe here, at least for tonight. I swear it. You've already warmed your cardboard up. *(She sits down, as does he.)*

JOSEPH. Like I said, biggest regret of me life as I got up and just walked out the door, in the middle of Christmas dinner.

MARIAN. I understand why you regret it but-

JOSEPH. Exactly! Biggest regret of me life I was thinking to meself as I walked out. So, I walked right back in there and bet the scrawny bastard black and fuckin blue. Fucked the turkey at him 'n all I did. *(Marian can't help but laugh.)* Wouldn't mind, poor Moira spent ages makin' the thing. Probably terrified master Derek wouldn't like it. He didn't like it in the end, I can tell ye. *(He mimes throwing a turkey at someone and their reaction.)* She was fucked off at me though, yeah. She was. It was up to her; she knew she could ask me to do it and I would have, but she didn't. Anyway, he was me landlord, which probably explains why she didn't approve of my actions. That was eight year ago, so here I am.

MARIAN. What happened to her?

JOSEPH. Ah, he got the picture and he left her ... ye know. We haven't spoke, me 'n her. I feel bad though.

MARIAN. After all this time?

JOSEPH. No, no, for you. I shouldn't have said that to your Derek. I shoulda asked. I can send him another call me and apologize for what I said to him, if you want? *(Marian starts laughing small and then large.)* What? Don't you think he'd accept my apology?

MARIAN. You kept callin' him a scrawny fucker.

JOSEPH. Is he not?

MARIAN. He's a fat cunt. He's about 16 stone.

JOSEPH. Little Derek huh? Oh, hang on! I forgot something. *(He goes to his bag.)* It's around here somewhere. *(He looks in the bag and stops for a second.)* Ah sure, I may as well. *(He puts the Santa hat back on and takes out a piece of paper).* Ho, Ho, Ho! The wi-fi code! *(He holds the paper up triumphantly.)* Do you know how to … eh … use it? *(Marian takes the wi-fi code and the phone and taps away.)*

MARIAN. There. Connected. How did you get the code?

JOSEPH. Ah, I come in here for a Brown Thomas, if you know what I mean? Best jacks in all of Dublin. I'd say the tissue paper is as expensive as their tea towels. Found a receipt on the floor. Had the code. Ten grand for a handbag? Can ye believe it?

MARIAN. Unfortunately, I can. Okay. I can do this.

JOSEPH. Ah yer not gonna call little Derek, are ye? I mean ye can do what you want …

MARIAN. My dad retired to Kerry. We haven't spoken in a long time …

JOSEPH. Ah he'd be delighted to hear from you.

MARIAN. And learn I'm a failure? Thirty years old, I'm supposed to have my shit together. I have a job, how did I let myself end up like this?

JOSEPH. No family in Dublin? *(She shakes her head.)* Friends? *(She shakes it again.)* You can't go back to your house?

MARIAN. He left-

JOSEPH. Good.

MARIAN. -a few months ago, and they changed the locks. I paid the rent; I just couldn't deal anymore, and I started ... spending what little I had on the drink. Just for a release. Just a little valve for the pressure. And look at me now. *(Joseph puts his arms out for a hug, she hesitates at first, but then goes towards him, accepting his invitation.)* What will he think of me now?

JOSEPH. He'll think he loves you and he has to be there for you. You are my responsibility, ye know?

MARIAN. What? Ah, no.

JOSEPH. And I'm yours. We're brother and sister in this country. Fuck Dublin. It's a tourist attraction now, for the rich. We're Irish. There is a failure here alright, but it's not you and it's not me. Do you hear me? It's not me and it's not you. Go on. Give him a ring. He'll be delighted.

MARIAN. Yeah. *(She makes the call.)* Dad? It's me. Yeah, I'm ok. *(She breaks.)* No. No, I'm not. *(Marian walks off-stage, crying, phone at her ear. Joseph looks at her.)*

JOSEPH. Really hope she doesn't leg it with me phone. *(He stretches out his sleeping bag again. He looks at the bottle of vodka and takes a sip. After a moment, Marian returns.)*

MARIAN. Joseph.

JOSEPH. Hope you don't mind; I should have asked ...

MARIAN. No. It's ok, you keep it.

JOSEPH. Did you get sorted?

MARIAN. Yeah, he's paying for a hotel and ... he's on the way up.

JOSEPH. That's a good father.

MARIAN. Yeah.

JOSEPH. And a good daughter.

MARIAN. Thanks. It was nice to meet you. *(She*

hands back the phone and puts a hand on his shoulder. She hesitates, then leaves.)

MARIAN O/S. Mind yourself.

JOSEPH. I will. *(Joseph cries. Alone again. The clock in the window behind him, strikes midnight. Fireworks can be heard in the distance.)*

JOSEPH. *(Sings)* Should auld acquaintance be forgot, and never brought to mind. Should auld acquaintance be forgot and the days of auld lang syne. *(Marian comes back and sits beside Joseph. Like a sibling. She joins in his song. Hand in hand.)*

JOSEPH/MARIAN
For auld lang syne,
my jo, for auld lang
syne,
we'll tak a cup o'
kindness yet, for auld
lang syne.
For auld lang syne,
my jo, for auld lang
syne,
we'll tak a cup o'
kindness yet, for auld
lang syne.

THE END

KEYBOARD WARRIORS

CHARACTERS

STEVIE. Young and energetic. Stevie is the new Pop Queen of the Irish e-sports scene. Graceful, patient and professional, she is aware of her image and how it is interpreted by her fans. As the play goes on, the facade falls to reveal something more real.

KAI. Late 20's, too old now for e-sports. A failed e-sports Olympic hopeful, Kai has taken to coaching and has taken Stevie under his wing.

J. Alcoholic, unpredictable, brazen and confident. J is operating under an anonymous name; she is a former Olympic e-sports champion, and now works freelance as an online assassin. Whilst being an artist at what she does, she takes no pleasure in it.

FRANKIE. Stevie's father and employer of J. An Irish developer and proud of his work. He is sick of Stevie wasting her life in an e-sports gym and hires J to annihilate her online presence.

ANNOUNCER. An over-the-top voice recording, reminiscent of a video game narrator.

TIME: Ireland Summer, 2029.

SCENE: *The stage is split in half. Stage right is STEVIE'S studio. There are posters in the background, depicting her most famous victories e.g. 'The Battle of Blanchardstown 2025', some fan art, depicting her online profile - 'STEVIEKICKSA$$', and a gaming chair in the centre of her studio. There are boxes of energy drinks dotted around and strategically placed with the logo towards the audience. Stage left is J's bedroom. Completely messy, clothes are tossed around, a mattress is on the floor, an almost drained drinks cabinet on the wall, stage left, and a matching chair. There is an Anarchy poster in the background. A French press is almost full of coffee beans and lies near a half empty bottle of whiskey, facing the audience. J sleeps on the mattress under a sleeping bag in her room, the lights are down.*

Lights up on Stevie's studio. She sits on the gaming chair, facing the audience. She is wearing a T-Shirt with various sponsorships from businesses on it and her username emblazoned across the front. Her coach, KAI, has the mirror image on a Hoodie. He wears a baseball cap with the word 'COACH' on it. She has a keyboard and mouse in front of her and is concentrating intently. Kai stands to her side and waves a towel to keep her cool.

KAI. Stay sharp. Stay sharp. You see him?
STEVIE. Yep.
KAI. Wait.
STEVIE. I got it.
KAI. Now! *(Stevie explodes into action on her keyboard and mouse, clicking and typing furiously.)* Pile it on! Pile it on!
STEVIE. Almost … there!
ANNOUNCER. V-V-V-Victory! *(Stevie and Kai jump in the air to celebrate.)*
STEVIE. Oh my God! Oh my God! We did it!
KAI. We did!
STEVIE. I'm in the All-Ireland Final! Oh God! Thank you … thank you, Coach!
KAI. Well done. Well done. *(They hug and then shake hands.)*
ANNOUNCER. D-D-D-Donation! *(Stevie turns to the computer.)*
STEVIE. Oh my God. I'm so grateful. *(She says 'hello everyone' in at least four languages)* Thank you so much for your support and your donation! I hope you tune in for the finals! *(She makes an excited gesture and puts her hands into a heart shape, reaches forward and turns off her live camera.)* Fuck! You were right, it's so hard not to curse online!
KAI. Those workshops totally paid off.
STEVIE. I was so close to calling him a f-
KAI. -Don't say it. Focus on the next round, we're going international. *(Lights down on Stevie's side of the stage and lights up on J's side. She is still asleep under the sleeping bag. Frankie bangs on her door.)*
FRANKIE. Hey! Hey! I know you're in there. *(J Groans.)*
J. I'm not.
FRANKIE. You definitely are. Come on, open up.

This place is a shit hole and I'm far too rich to be waiting out here.

J. Piss off.

FRANKIE. Piss off? Maybe I should just knock on your neighbour's doors until I find some other loser who's wasted their life on videogames to take my bit credits for a simple job. Remember those? *(J stumbles up and lets Frankie into her space. He is disgusted with the surroundings.)*

FRANKIE. Lovely interior decor. Love the smell. Quite … musty.

J. I want double what you offered.

FRANKIE. Double? Forget it.

J. Triple.

FRANKIE. You can't just double the amount every time I speak.

J. Quadruple. *(Frankie stands tall and purposely says nothing. J swigs from a bottle of whiskey.)* Or you can try your luck banging on doors in the ghetto here and see if anyone else is able to do what I can do … without stabbing you in the eye and robbing you blind, of course.

FRANKIE. Maybe I will. Surely there's a lot more like you out there, at a more reasonable price. *(J hands Frankie something.)*

FRANKIE. What's this?

J. My E-Olympic Gold medal. Go door to door and see if anyone else has one.

FRANKIE. It's just a piece of metal.

J. Who are you telling.

FRANKIE. Double.

J. Triple.

FRANKIE. Double and a half.

J. Double and two halves. Half up front, and half on completion.

FRANKIE. Fine. *(He uses his smartphone and makes*

a sweeping gesture on it. J swings up from the bed.)
J. Who's the target?
FRANKIE. My daughter. I want you to annihilate her, humiliate her, and destroy her.
J. Such a loving father.
FRANKIE. I want you to make it, so she doesn't end up like you.
J. What's wrong with being me? *(Frankie looks around the pigsty of a 'home'.)* Fair point. What's her handle? *(Frankie looks at his smartphone.)*
FRANKIE. It's 'Stevie kicks A, dollar, dollar. *(J shakes her head and types on her keyboard.)*
J. Found her. Oh. She's in the All-Ireland Final. Surprisingly good performance.
FRANKIE. Is she?? The All-Ireland Final? Ah no if she wins that she'll only get encouraged. Can you somehow get in there and do your thing?
J. Like suddenly qualify and enter the All-Ireland Final without even qualifying and earning my spot in the final?
FRANKIE. Yeah.
J. Hang on. *(She types.)*
J. I can actually, yeah. You just need to bump up the last-minute entry fee.
FRANKIE. How much is it? *(She points to the 'screen'.)* Fuck off, that's extortion.
J. Yep. *(She takes another slug from her whiskey. Lights down on J's side. Lights up on Stevie's.)*
ANNOUNCER. Challenger D-D-D-Donation!
STEVIE. Oh, wow! Another one! Thank you, thank you-
KAI. That's not for you.
STEVIE. What?
KAI. Someone's challenging the finalists. They've offered a wager … woah …
STEVIE. A wager for that much?

KAI. We should take it.

STEVIE. But … I don't care about the money.

KAI. Yeah, but I care about my twenty percent.

STEVIE. What?

KAI. Nothing. *(Beat.)* That's a lot of money Stevie. It's more than the All- Ireland prize money, it's ridiculous.

STEVIE. Being champion isn't about the money. *(Long beat.)*

KAI. Okay. Okay. You're right. Well, it's too late now anyway-

ANNOUNCER. Challenge A-A-A-Accepted!

KAI. Shit.

STEVIE. What?

KAI. It's my former student.

STEVIE. J? Oh Jesus. She's an Olympic Gold medallist. A super e-athlete. The first female to win-

KAI. It doesn't matter, we've got to focus. *(He takes her by the shoulders and turns her to the 'screen').* She's got to get through the other finalist first. Observe how she's playing, at least we'll have time to figure out some strategies and pick her patterns and predict her …

ANNOUNCER. T-T-T-Total Victoryyyyy. Annihalation. Humiliation. D-D-D-D-Destructiiiioooon. *(Kai and Stevie both gulp.)*

ANNOUNCER. J advances to the final. *(Lights up on J's side. Frankie has his arms crossed and is observing coldly.)*

J. What's up, shit face?

STEVIE. Eh, excuse me?

J. Not you, loser. Your loser coach.

KAI. What's up, J?

J. Nothing. Just been hired to assassinate your little protégé. I've watched her highlights. How basic, and that fake personality? You disgust me.

STEVIE. I'm not fake. I'm the same online as I am in person. (*J scoffs. Frankie 'takes the mic' by leaning into the audience.*)

FRANKIE. Stevie, just quit now okay, I've hired this washed-up Olympic champ, she just smashed the other finalist in-

J. -Record time.

FRANKIE. Yeah, record time. I'm sure whoever 'Buttkicker9000' was, is at home crying into his cereal or something.

J. Most likely.

FRANKIE. If you don't want the same thing to happen to you, just quit the game, go outside and go find a real job.

KAI. E-sports athlete is a real job in 2039, pal!

FRANKIE. The only athlete I smell around here is athlete's foot, mate.

STEVIE. Dad, I can't believe you'd try to do this to me.

J. Excuse me? Try? Oh, I'd nearly do this for free.

FRANKIE. Would you?

J. Figure of speech.

ANNOUNCER. Round one C-C-C-Commencing!

STEVIE. Oh my, look at all of those who zoned in to watch! (*She makes her heart gesture*). Thank you so much for your words of encouragement. I'd like to wish my new challenger all the best and may the best gamer win. I've got to put my game face on now so talk soon! (*She kisses for the camera. Kai massages her hands and shoulders quickly*).

J. You make me sick.

STEVIE. Can't handle people being nice?

J. You remind me of me, and I hate myself.

FRANKIE. Get this over with.

ANNOUNCER. Get ready- F-F-F-Fight! (*Stevie and J both type extremely fast on their keyboards. Stevie*

concentrates intensely, J looks bored.)
KAI. You've got her on the run. Keep going. *(J whispers to Frankie who reluctantly taps his phone.)*
ANNOUNCER. L-L-L-Loot box. *(Stevie and Kai look at each other, worried. J brings her finger up into the air and down on the keyboard. We hear an explosion noise.)*
ANNOUNCER. N-N-N-N-Nuke. Nuke. Nuke. Winner! *(Frankie goes to high five J but it is brutally rejected.)*
STEVIE. She can't just do that! Can she? She paid for the loot box and got the nuke …
KAI. Once she bought her way in … once that money is paid, it never ends. They just want more and more.
STEVIE. Hey J!
J. Yes, sugar plum?
STEVIE. I thought Olympic medals were all about honour, fair play and sportsmanship … not cheating.
J. If it were cheating, it wouldn't be in the game.
STEVIE. When you won your gold medal, were loot boxes a thing?
KAI. No, they weren't.
STEVIE. So why are you using them now?
J. Because you've got to do whatever it takes to win. Isn't that right, coach?
FRANKIE. It sure is.
J. Not you.
KAI. Whatever it takes, yeah.
STEVIE. I almost had you in that round. Are you too scared to face me without loot boxes?
J. No, not at all. It's just quicker with them and I get paid faster and can get back to my life.
STEVIE. But this is my life. I've been training for this for years. Surely, you'd understand what that's

like?

J. Look. Believe me, I hate to say it, kid. Your dad's right. Ugh, makes me feel sick.

FRANKIE. You sure that's not the vodka? Or the smell?

J. Go out and get a real job. Don't listen to sleazebag losers that want to live vicariously through you.

KAI. I didn't want to live vicariously through you.

J. Stop, you tried to take all the credit as the best coach ever, just admit you can't do what I can do. You never could.

KAI. You know you only have an athletic life from nine to twenty-two, and it's all downhill from there. Reaction times. Eyesight. Testosterone.

STEVIE. What?

KAI. Well, maybe not that last one.

STEVIE. I'm twenty-five.

J. And I'm older again and I'm kicking your protégé's ass.

ANNOUNCER. R-R-R-Round two.

STEVIE. Oh no! She's got the loot boxes and-

FRANKIE. -and my money, Stevie. You're not gonna win! Just forfeit now. I'll make it worth your while.

ANNOUNCER. D-D-D-Donation for Stevie!

STEVIE. What?

KAI. What?

STEVIE. Oh? Thank you! (*She says thank you in three different languages as the donations roll in. She makes her heart gesture, J launches furiously into her keyboard, she's not bored anymore. Frankie furiously taps his phone, donating to J.*)

ANNOUNCER. D-D-D-Donation for J!

FRANKIE. Aren't you gonna say thanks?

J. Shut up, I'm concentrating. (*She takes a swig of her whiskey as she types. Kai is leaping about excited.*)

Stevie stands as she types, knowing she has J on the run.)

ANNOUNCER. W-W-W-Winner - Stevie!! Kaaaa-aaaayyyyy Ooooooooooooh yeeeaaaaahhh! *(Stevie stands up and blows her hair out of her face.)*

STEVIE. Looks like we got ourselves an even playing field now! *(She turns to the camera.)* Thank you so much to my generous donators!! Are you ready to see some more?

J. I wouldn't be so confident if I was you.

STEVIE. I'd just like to say, what an honour it is to face a former Olympic gold medallist in my first All-Ireland Final! Cuddles and loves to everyone watching!

J. Fuck this.

ANNOUNCER. R-R-R-R-Round three! M-M-M-M-Montaaaaage!! *(Electronic dance music plays as a montage plays out on stage. Kai feeds energy drinks to Stevie through a straw as she types away. Frankie folds his arm in mock disdain, but then looks over his shoulder, more interested than he would like to let on. A bell is rung for a break and Kai massages Stevie's hands. Frankie starts massaging J's shoulders but is rejected as J eats a bowl of cereal. The bell rings again.)*

ANNOUNCER. D-D-D-Donation montage! *(Cash register noises play over and over.)* Donation for Stevie! D-D-Donation for J! D-D-D-Donation Nation!!

STEVIE. It's an even playing field now.

J. Careful what you wish for. *(Both players lean forward intently, hammering away at the keyboard and mouse. Random letters and bits fall off them. Steam comes out of both the keyboards.)*

FRANKIE. How much money is that? In ten minutes of playing …

KAI. That has got to be a record amount of money. *(Kai's phone rings in his pocket. He answers it.)*
KAI. Yes? Hello? Yes, I'm her manager. Plus twenty percent. That twenty percent is for me. Yes, yes, yes, we accept those terms, yes! I'll just get her fingerprint when I get a chance. *(Kai moves towards Stevie's furiously moving fingers.)*
FRANKIE. She's actually really good at this, isn't she?
J. Shut the fuck up, I'm trying to concentrate. *(Stevie is sweating with steely focus in her eyes. Kai can't get her to 'sign' the agreement.)*
ANNOUNCER. V-V-Victory!!! NEW ALL IRELAND CHAMPIIIIIIIIYYYYYYYYYYAAAAAAAA-AAAWWWWWWWNNNNNN! *(Stevie stands up, straight as an arrow, and smashes her headset on the floor.)*
STEVIE. Yes! Take that, you fucking CUNT! *(A dead heavy silence in both rooms.)* Oh no. *(Kai springs into action and tries to get Stevie's fingerprint on his phone.)*
ANNOUNCER. SP-SP-SP-SPONSORSHIP DENIII-IIIED! C-WORD C-WORD C-WORD!!! D-D-D-DO-NATION DENIED! CLICK-BAIT ARTICLE. CLICK BAIT ARTICLE. OPINION PIECE. COMMENTS. COMMENTS. COMMENTS. HASHTAG CANCEL STEVIE. CANCELLATION COMPLETE! TOTAL! CAREER! DESTRUUUUUUUUCCCCCCTIIIIIIION!!!! *(Stevie picks up her headset and speaks into it.)*
STEVIE. Woops! Hi, everyone. Sorry about that.
ANNOUNCER. Apology ABSOLUTELY NOT accepted-ed-ed!
STEVIE. Thank you so much for the support, I-
ANNOUNCER. SUPPORT LOST. ANNIHALATION-LATION-LATION.
KAI. That was EA on the phone. They wanted to

sponsor you. The biggest sponsorship deal in the world. You wrecked it.

STEVIE. I wrecked it? I won the All-Ireland, I beat a world and Olympic champion and I wrecked it?

KAI. Look at all the support you lost.

FRANKIE. And the money. I mean … it'd take you years of a real job to build that up again, I-

STEVIE. This is my real job-

J. Was-

STEVIE. Was my real job. In my real life. It's all I ever wanted to do. Nothing else made me happier … support? From you? *(To Kai)* I can do the things you can never do.

J. Preach, sister.

KAI. I taught you everything.

STEVIE. No, you didn't. I already knew everything you taught me.

KAI. I gave you access to the tournaments.

STEVIE. Does that make you something more than me? You gate keeper. You keep kids like me out of the game because you've got it sewn up and you want to control people like me. My image, the way I speak …

KAI. I came round to the way you speak.

STEVIE. I like being nice. I like being positive on-line. There's so much hate on it, you told me it wasn't going to work.

KAI. And look where you are now.

STEVIE. It was one little mistake.

KAI. Whoever makes the first mistake loses, and in your case, you lost fuckin' big.

STEVIE. Get out, 'coach'. Just get out.

KAI. I'd say we could get over this in a few years, but-

STEVIE. But I'm too old?

KAI. You're officially a washed-up loser.

FRANKIE. Don't you talk to my daughter like that! Stevie, you did so well. I'm coming over, stay there-

STEVIE. No. You stay away too. All of a sudden, you're supporting me? Where were you the last three years? Since Damien got sick? I took a leaf out of your book and sat at the computer all day. Working. Getting good. I tried and I tried to show you how good I was. He loved seeing me do well, but you never …

FRANKIE. I didn't think it was real, Stevie. it's not the same as the stock market.

STEVIE. It was real to me. It was my life. I don't have anything else. Not even a dad. A brother. Or a friend. Get out! *(Kai leaves, Stevie puts her head in her hands and cries.)*

FRANKIE. I'm on the way, Stevie, OK, we can fix this.

J. Before you go. The money.

FRANKIE. Yeah. Yeah. Here. *(J puts her fingerprint on the phone. Cash register sound goes off.)* Hey. Well played. *(She nods. Frankie leaves.)*

J. Oh, you've no idea. Hey, kid. You still there?

STEVIE. Hey.

J. You really like this e-sports shit?

STEVIE. It's not shit.

J. Your coach just wants your money, and your dad's not much better.

STEVIE. Yeah.

J. So why do it for them?

STEVIE. I don't.

J. Oh, you do it for yourself, the honour, the prestige.

STEVIE. Yeah, and someone else. Here. *(She waves her finger up on her phone and J gets a message.)*

J. Fan mail? Really?

STEVIE. It was my first ever donation.

J. Ten credits. In 2025, after the coronavirus? That was a lot of money back then. 'Dear Stevie, thanks so much for playing videogames with me all week. The hospital is pretty boring, but everyone here is really nice, which makes it easier. I'm glad we can play online because sometimes I pretend that you're here beside me, sometimes even when I'm not playing games. I still can't believe you beat the final boss on your first go. You're the best ever. I think you should go professional. Don't be hard on Dad, he's just playing 'Crypto' to get us money for when I'm out of here. I'm gonna beat this virus, like you beat final bosses. Here's your first donation. Can't wait to see you win a World Championship. Love you. Damien'. Who's Damien?

STEVIE. My baby brother.

J. You think of him when you play?

STEVIE. I think of the virus. It makes me play extra hard, I imagine every time I win, he gets a bit better, and I try and be nice coz it made a difference to him. That fucking …

J. That fucking cunt of a virus?

STEVIE. Yeah.

J. No wonder you're so good. (*J taps a few keys into the keyboard.*)

ANNOUNCER. D-D-D-DONATION REVIEWED. 10 DOLLARS. FR-R-R-R-R-OM JAAAAAYYYYYYY-YYY. FRIENDSHIP UNLOCKED.

J. Rumour has it, you're looking for a new coach?

STEVIE. You?

J. It's hard to beat a virus on your own. You need a team.

STEVIE. I'm sorry I called you a c-word.

J. You didn't. Even if you did, I forgive you.

ANNOUNCER. FORGIVENESS ACHIEVED! SPON-SORSHIP OPEN! SPONSORSHIP OPEN!

J. You know the European qualifiers are next week? *(Stevie panics and gets all her equipment together.)*

STEVIE. We've got to get practicing.

J. No! No. No. We've got to go for a drink. It's on your dad anyway. How many drinks can half a million cryptos get you these days?

STEVIE. A lot? *(She waves on her phone.)*

J. See you here in half an hour?

STEVIE. Okay. Computer shut down. Shut down. Close. Turn off. Off. *(Stevie rips the plug out of the socket, just as Frankie comes into the room.)*

FRANKIE. Did you quit? *(Stevie looks at the plug, then her dad.)*

STEVIE. I don't know. *(She walks off the stage. Frankie looks at the computer.)*

FRANKIE. I never knew you were that good.

THE END

MONOLOGUES

If you're starting your journey as an actor, you need some tools in your toolbox. A good place to start is a decent monologue. One that suits you, that speaks to you and gets a reaction out of you when you first read it. These monologues are designed as self-contained pieces. Some of them first featured in the Fireside monologue challenge 2020. You can use these monologues to add to your showreel, to help you audition or if you just want to stay sharp and practice and have fun with some text that is new to you. I only ask that if you are putting your performance online publicly that you credit me as the writer. Change the genders as necessary, you'll notice the characters are often just called 'character' for this reason. It is you who brings words to life after all. I hope you enjoy, and I wish you all the best on your journey.

A SUMMONING OF SORTS

The character has been tormented by a teenager driving up and down their council estate at all hours of the day and night. In desperation they summon a demon to help them with their nuisance. It worked … a little too well.

CHARACTER. Look, I'm sorry alright. What do you mean that doesn't cut it? Isn't this what this is about? 'If you hurt someone else, you're only hurting yourself?'. A journey of self-discovery and admitting yeah … I probably shouldn't have wished for that. Yeah, yeah, I've learned my lesson. Yes, I know what I've wished for but … look at him. Look. You exploded his head. I didn't think you'd do that. There's bits all over the road, on the bike, Oh, great here come the Gards. Finally! He can do wheelies up the road all day and they never come but the second, the instant, his head explodes they're on the way!1 Yeah, I know what I said. I said I know what I said. *(Long beat)* Okay, I asked *you* for help- yes- summoned you, okay, summoned you, with the Ouija board and everything, whatever- to *get rid of a nuisance*. He's up and down the road at all hours on his scrambler, frightening the neighbours, frightening me Nan, frightenin'… me. *(beat)* No! there was absolutely no justification in exploding his head!! I refuse to believe there wasn't a more … diplomatic way of dealing with this. Of course, I asked him to stop he told me to fuck off hence I summoned you. *(beat)* Oh. There really was no other way was there? No? Ok. So how do I get you back in the Ouija board?

APPRAISAL

The WHITE ANGEL is in a meeting for her Centenary appraisal. She/he been tasked with guiding humanity for the last thousand years.

WHITE ANGEL. Two out of ten for friendliness? Two out of ten? No, I don't agree with that. Not at all. Two? Surely the humans are friendlier than that? Mother Theresa? Live Aid? Well, the money probably didn't end up where it was supposed to … Jesus? Was Jesus in the last appraisal? That was twenty out of ten that time, yeah you couldn't say feck all to me then. Oh right, the crucifixion. Well, that's not in the last thousand years anyway. The atom bomb was a once off! Well … twice … third times a charm, eh? *(Beat)* Climate change? Sure, that's just the internet, it was global freezing the eighties and now it's global warming. The internet. The feckin' internet. Everything was perfectly fine before the internet came along. Why am I being judged on the internet? I didn't invent it. You should be bringing robots in and giving them their appraisal. Robots ... are they gonna replace us do you think?

CALL ME DONALD

MURPHY is in the gym and approaches a fellow gym goer. He has been plagued by a recurring dream and is looking for help.

MURPHY. Do you visualize? Do you plan your dreams out? Like those tony Robbins books? Okay. Cool, yeah, I do. I do a lot. Do you get, like, recurring dreams when you're doing the visualization exercises? Like I'm doing the power pose, 'strength' right? Then I relax and I close my eyes and I walk around my ideal house. You know? Like we're supposed to vividly imagine. I walk into the bathroom, gold everywhere, huge ornate mirrors, six-foot jacuzzi that I'm just about to step into and I smell

something. Vividly. I look over and, on the jacks ... naked ... taking a nasty shit ... is the President of the United States. This is my visualisation. Like this is my ideal house it's supposed to be mine. The books say I've got to see it to believe it. I've got to meditate on it. I just can't get him out of my mind. In the visualisation, he sees me! He makes direct eye contact, he stares right through me as if to say - 'Nice bathroom, it's mine now' and he stands up, he doesn't even wipe! He puts his hand out and I shake it! Why do I shake it? He squeezes my hand with both hands and says, "Call me Donald". Does that happen to you?

CHARLIE'S GREATEST FEAR

CHARLIE gave away their soul.

CHARLIE. What scares you? Not that shit that goes bump in the night. What's your greatest fear? That's what they're going to ask you. If I were a generous person, I'd tell you not to answer that. I'd tell you that as soon as you tell someone that, you tell them you deepest, most secret … hope. Then they own you. They do. From the inside out. They know, what it is, that scares you so much it shrivels your heart into a withered useless chunk of flesh. Do you know how full of pain hope is? How useless it is? It's like drinking gallons of saltwater and expecting your thirst to disappear. What's my greatest fear? No, I don't fear anymore. *(Long beat.)* I was afraid of the dark. I already told them. It's too late for me. I hoped … *(long beat)* I hope you never tell them. *(Charlie looks to the door as footsteps approach.)* They're coming … for you.

CULT LEADER

The CHARACTER despises what they believe to be weakness and yet needs it to survive.

CULT LEADER. You know that deep down feeling that tells you you're wrong? Not that *you're* wrong about something but that you, *you* are wrong. I can't cure that, but I tell you I can, and you lap it up like a dog because I am charismatic, welcoming, inquisitive. *(Beat)* I ask you things you wish people would ask you. Then I tell you about your problems, in all honesty I make them up. They're not problems. You only think they are because you think you're a problem. Just to be clear it's me and only me that has the answer to these problems, and you will follow me to the ends of the earth to solve them for you. For you. To solve you for you. Such a marvellous gift. Thank you. I'll let you in on a secret … there is no answer to the problems I produce. Do you see how that works? I inspire you to believe in something, me for example, but I never inspire you to believe in the only thing you should … I am your cult leader, and I didn't even choose this for myself. You did. Oh, you can find me all over the world, anywhere there's authority and I mean anywhere and everywhere. Don't believe me? Doesn't matter. You're wrong. Remember that. Let me help you, for you.

FAMILY

The CHARACTER is a member of a gang accused of terrorizing a community.

CHARACTER. They're not *like* family to me they *are* my family. They look after me. When I came here, I was completely alone. Yeah, he started a fight with me. Came up to me and just started on me. He hit me but I've had worse, much worse, so I hit him back. He was supposed to be some big shot back then 'n I sparked him. They weren't his mate anymore. Heard he works in a bank now. Stealing? Come on. We'd never steal. Yer man who works in the bank he's probably stealin' right now. Someone would just find a car and we'd all be in the field bouncin' it to turn it around. We could only go forward. That was me first driving lesson 'til the Gards showed up. We'd get chased and we made sure none of us would get caught. And if any-one started row with us, they'd get it back straight away. We'd look out for each other, like I said. If one of us is attacked we're all attacked, and we'd make sure there'd be payback. I look out for them and they look out for me. That's family.

FREE HUGS

A random hug changed this CHARACTER'S life.

CHARACTER. When will this all be over so I can just grab a stranger in the street and hug them? A big hug. A strong one. The kind of hug that changes your life. Like the one I got on my way to work. Got off the Luas, Headphones on, drowning in my own head. I saw this group of lunatics outside Stephen's Green, big happy smiles, waving signs, singing songs, some of them were dancing. At seven o'clock in the morning? She was already on top of me by the time I saw the sign. Free Hugs. This stranger, big lady, not big physically but big spiritually. If you're lucky you know the type. All I could see was her hair, all I could smell was her, all I could feel was … warm. She squeezed me and she squeezed me. That morning I was trying to figure out what the best way to kill myself was. She squeezed that thought right out of me. So yeah, I miss hugs.

GIFTED

CHARACTER is an obsessed genius.

CHARACTER. People say I'm gifted. It annoys me. Truth is they're the ones with the gift. They can relax and be content with their miserable lives, their lives peaked long ago and it's not that they don't realize it, they do, it's too painful for them to admit it so they trap that feeling within themselves, put it under lock and key and drop it right into the very depths of their soul. I could never do that. It's the gift they give themselves. I'm a slave to perfection. I've got to strive to break barriers every single day and every single day I get closer to the secrets of the universe. I don't understand why others don't understand me. What else is there to do in life? Mate? Reproduce. Die? No, I'll leave that to them. They can numb themselves to the truth … I need it. The perfection.

GOODBYE PLAYER 2

The CHARACTER loves video games as much as they fear funerals.

CHARACTER. Starlight defenders two is the best video game in the world of all time. Ever. It's an absolute masterpiece. Miyamoto Kashiwazaki? Have you heard of him? Seen his posters on my wall? He said this is his Magnum Opus. You can customize your characters down to their fingernails ... and their genitals but that's- I'm not interested in that. The story is meant to be amazing. It's really immersive and your character can live forever, think of the possibilities. Yeah, I know he's dead. Sorry, he's passed away. Do I really have to go? Really? I don't think he'd mind. He'd want me to play this. He loves Starlight Defenders as much as I do. He's my player 2. There are a hundred and twenty-five gigabytes left to download. It's nearly here if we turn off everything that's using the wi-fi. Really? I've been waiting on this for years and he'll be dead forever. *(Long beat.)* He's really dead, isn't he? And he's not coming back. He was only online a few days ago.

GOOD LAD

CHARACTER is an MMA fighter in the dressing room warming up before their big fight.

CHARACTER. I'm not meant for this world. This time anyway. Suits, nine-to-fives and death. I'd be more comfortable smashing some heads on a battlefield with an axe or something. That's what my coach says. 'Good lad', he calls me. That's my fighting name, ye know? 'In the red corner with an undefeated record ... Good Lad!' I'm undefeated because the amateur record doesn't matter when you turn Pro, ye know? Turnin' pro this weekend. Wipin' the slate clean. I was bullied as a kid, relentlessly, I have to hand it to their relentlessness. Every day twice a day. They used to call me gay. That stopped when I my coach taught me how to fight. They couldn't call me that anymore because that would mean they were battered ... relentlessly ... by a gay. Good lad. Fuckers bought tickets to me fight.

I have to thank them though. If they didn't bully me, I'd never have learned how to fight ... I'd never be good lad.

GRAND THEFT AUTO

The CHARACTER reminisces on a simple, but life changing experience.

CHARACTER. It was 3:30 am. I had been playing it for most of the day I had school in the morning you know but who cared? Twenty hours it took to download, I kept checking every five mins. 'A watched kettle never boils' me granny shouts into me. She bought it for me. The game. I didn't even know she knew what a PlayStation voucher was. To this day it's my favourite birthday present, not the gift just the memory. 'Grand theft auto' she says. She tells me that's what my Uncle Wayne got done for in the States. He was the best. Paid more attention to me than my own da, who wasn't much better. My da used to boast about being out of prison ten years before they put him back in for five. I'm running people over in the game. The graphics were amazing, you can really feel the crunch when you run over a pedestrian ... and I felt sick. The game doesn't force you to do that, it's just a choice. That's when it all hit me. I'm being looked after by the most generous woman in the world. This 70-year-old who's raising me on her own because of the choices Father figures like my da and Uncle Charlie made. I put the PlayStation away that day. I went to school. I hated it; I really did but I made some different choices from that day on.

HAVE YOU GOT A SMOKE?

The CHARACTER sees abundance all around him but experiences none.

CHARACTER. Here. Have you got a smoke I could borrow? Have you got a smoke? That is such a fuckin' lie. Fuckin' liar. How hard is it to get one poxy smoke off someone in this city? All I'm askin' for is one of them smokes in that box of smokes I just seen you put away … in the inside pocket in your very warm looking jacket. I only asked for a lend of one anyway. What are you looking at me like that for? What are you looking at me like that for? Like that. That stupid scared look on your face. You look like … what do you look like? I know. You look as if I'm about to smash your face into that expensive window because you won't give me a poxy, worthless, little smoke. I wouldn't do anything like that to a stranger. See, I'm a much more generous person than you are … and I don't have anything to give. Not even a smoke.

HE DOES THE PUNCHING

Having been bullied in the past, the CHARACTER is terrified of the long-term effects of bullying that their son is currently experiencing.

CHARACTER. He is getting a punch bag. You don't like violence? Yeah, neither does he, have you seen him lately? The black eyes, bruises on his arm and when's the last time you heard him speak without being spoken to? Violence? Life is violent. What's going to happen next if he doesn't put a stop to this now? He'll go through life taking beatings left, right and centre. He'll settle for what he thinks he deserves, he'll settle in love for someone that beats him, someone that thinks

they're so superior every high and mighty word from their condescending mouth can hurt as much as a punch in the gut. *(Beat.)* My son deserves the world. He's getting a punch bag and he's going to punch it until his knuckles bleed and his arms and his heart hurts with the pain. Then he's going to put that pain straight

into a bully's face and break his nose. If that doesn't work, he's going to do it again, and again and again until everyone in the world realises my son is no punching bag. He does the punching.

I'LL TEXT YOU TOMORROW

The CHARACTER feels empty no matter how hard they try not to.

CHARACTER. I don't want to go. No. James, I don't want to go. You'll just leave me alone like last time and go chat with everyone and everyone will be talking to you because they're so happy to see you but not me. I'll be alone leaning on a wall with the same bottle of beer for the whole night half smiling at people I don't know … or like. I don't know how long I can keep this up for … being in your shadow. You've got this amazing job, amazing friends and amazing smile. I think you're amazing. What do I have? I'm going home. *(Long bea.t)* To make a decision. I'll text you tomorrow.

IT'S NOT ABOUT
THE CAT

The character is a psychopath.

CHARACTER. It's not about the cat, is it? No, it's not. You always do this. You always try and make me out to be a monster. Am I that bad? Really, am I? Look at me and tell me? No. Silence. So, what is it then? It's not dead. How could you even accuse me of doing something like that? You never put the bins out last night. You never did. I had to do it. Do you know how much of an embarrassment it is to have to take the bins out when I'm in my dressing gown? Everyone's watching me. I can feel their eyes burning into me. It is about the bins. For the last time I don't fucking care about the cat. Do you think I care about it enough that I'd risk everything just to wring its neck? It probably climbed into the fucking brown bin again. *(Beat.)* Oh.

JUST SAY YES

The Character is an addict.

CHARACTER. I blame the schools. I totally and utterly blame the schools. That was the most incompetent, stupid thing, ever to do to a kid. I remember them saying, "Don't do it. Just say no." Say no to what? What are they talking about, I thought we had a history class this morning? Who's yer wan come in to talk to us. What's she talkin' about? Oh, drugs? she did a load of drugs? What are they? 'They give them out at parties and they're really dangerous'. Sorry, yeah, I only heard the first half of that sentence. They give them out at parties? Where are these parties? Jaysus, there seems to be a lot of parties going around. How do you get an invite to these parties? Ye know? Me and my friends like parties. It was Jennie's birthday party last week, we had cake and you're tellin' me we coulda had drugs? 'Here's a list of all the drugs you have to say no to'. Mushrooms? My Ma loves mushrooms with the dinner. I'm nine years old and my droning, nasal talking, posh, condescending, uncool teacher is telling me not to do drugs. That he doesn't do drugs. That if I want to grow up to be like him then I won't do them. Of course, that's only gonna make me want to do them more. Why did they get the most un-coolest person in the world to tell us he thought drugs were uncool? He should have said "Just say yes". Then guess what? None of us would have wanted to do 'em! Pricks. Anyway, I've a party to keep going.

JUSTICE

Kennedy sports a black eye and sits opposite two others.

KENNEDY. Evenin' lads, lady. Do you want me to start my report? (long beat) Right. He was a fucking scumbag. How is it justice that one fella can hold an entire community to ransom, we pick him up (beat). Doesn't matter that we never picked him up, the judge would just let him out to do it all again. That place is full of good, genuine, hardworking people. Salt of the earth, like my da was, like your ma was. People like them havin' to deal with pricks like him? While we sit back and do nothin'? Justice? Going up and down all hours of the morning on his poxy scrambler that he got for Christmas from his drug pushing Ma. I don't care if he's eleven years old. He could be a hundred years old, and I'd still do what I done. He won't be in a hurry to hop on that bike again let me tell ye. Justice.

LAST NIGHT

The Character playfully approaches their on again/off again love interest.

CHARACTER. What happened last night? Oh, I know what happened I just want you to say it. Yeah, I just think it would be better if you said it. Well, there was a half cleaned eh … stain behind the curtain, the bleach is still there and … tissue paper. I'm a little more than certain that was me. Yeah, I found your bra on the extractor fan. I'll get it for you in a bit, but I think we kissed. Again. Last night. No before we had the moo-moos. Mimosas? Mimosas … and tequila and Guinness. Yeah, I know you only had one. Yeah, I think you … I got sick. I got sick yeah that was me too. Do you want an aspirin? So, the kiss. Are we … are we back together now? Coz I'd really like that … if you did. No, I don't mind all that, drunk adults are just like sleepy toddlers. Yeah. Speaking of toddlers there was a pregnancy test in the bathroom last time you were here, and it was positive.

ONE BROTHER

The Character sits in front of an easel and paints a landscape. He carefully brushes the paint brush on the canvas.

CHARACTER. I always wanted to paint. My Father used to say that shit was fairies so that was the end of that. He taught me and Jeff how to shoot, how to hunt... and how to take a punch. I could always take it better than Jeff. The older brother's cross to bear. He used to tell everyone that he enlisted as some patriotic calling or duty. It was bullshit. He knew war was safer than staying at home ... with him. *(He puts the paintbrush down and observes his work.)* The scenery is different without the helicopters. It is beautiful. You don't get a chance to take it all in when you're there you don't get a chance. You don't get a chance ... *(He takes up the brush again, but this time holds it like a knife.)* He called me bro. That prick at the bar. I fucking hate it. I hate it when someone calls me bro. You never fucking earned the right to be my brother. You haven't been through what we've been through. What makes you think you're my brother? I've only one brother ... *(He stabs the painting ferociously ruining all his good work.)* ... and I left him over there.

ONE PUNCH

The Character is being interviewed, again, by police.

CHARACTER. I've told you already so many times. *(Beat.)* Fine. Inside the club he was harassing Jemma. Putting his arm around her waist and I told, I asked him, to stop. To leave her alone- I think it's important. *(Beat.)* It is important because it justifies- explains, what happened outside. *(Beat.)* Yeah, so we got out coats and went out. We didn't put them on because it was a hot summers night. He followed us. He followed Jemma and he tried again. I … spoke to him again- yes, I know you have it on CCTV that's what I'm doing there.

Speaking to him. Then he raised his fist. He was going to hit me. Hit her. I was afraid, I had to act fast. It was one punch, I threw it before I thought about it. The size of him, I didn't think he'd … I never hit someone before in my life. His head hit the concrete and it just turned my stomach. I just wanted to get out of there so I took Jemma. No. She didn't come with me. She stayed. It was just one punch. It was self-defence, that's all it was. One punch.

PERFECTLY ADEQUATE

The CHARACTER has been adequately married for years.

CHARACTER. He keeps cooking for me. It's not nice, it's an imposition is what it is. It is. I never ask him to and now whenever and whatever he cooks I've got to eat. Baking now as well he is. Apple tarts, cup-cakes, Halloween brack? It's fuckin' February. The apple tarts are nice though I like them. He knows I'm on a diet and I'm exercising every morning. 'You don't need to exercise, you're perfect'. Yeah, and you're perfectly adequate, Thomas. Perfectly adequate husband with a perfectly adequate job and a perfectly, social life and perfectly adequate sex. That's what me ma said about him on our wedding day. You've found yourself a perfectly adequate match darling. *(Long beat.)* What a bitch. Well, maybe I want more than a perfectly adequate life. *(Beat.)* Or husband.

PHANTOM LIMBS

The CHARACTER'S house is haunted, so they called a paranormal investigative team.

CHARACTER. There's something in the basement. I felt something touching my leg down there. It rubbed my calf. It felt nice. They say this place used to be a doctor's surgery back in the day. Like a hundred years ago. Back when they chopped your arm off if you had nightmares. Or blood poisoning, whatever. There are rumours there are body parts buried in different parts of the back garden. I was sunbathing during the summer and something slapped my ass. Have you heard of disembodied voices? I've heard them, in the last place I lived. Phantom limbs? Yep. That's what I think is haunting me here. I think the spirits of these limbs are jealous of my body. When I got out of the shower last week, I got a kick in the crotch and I heard a disembodied voice laugh at me. Yeah, I called a priest but that only
made it worse. He got a slap across the face as soon as he went into the bedroom. He wouldn't answer my phone calls so that's why I called you. Can you help? Thank you. Thanks. Oh, my insurance company said I should get you to sign these waivers in case you get a physical injury.

PUB?

The Character goes to AA for the first and only time.

CHARACTER. Yeah, my name's … well, I don't wanna give my name. Jim, I guess. That'll do. Jim'll fix it, no, no he won't he definitely won't. Jim'll fuck it up. That's who I am. Eh … it's been twenty-eight relatively pain free hours since my last drink. Although sixteen of them were spent sleeping it off. So … do we still count it if we just sleep it off? I mean staying sober is easy when you're asleep. Just put yourself in a coma … quickest way to do that? *(Mimes drinking. Points to a member of the circle).* Not a good idea for you, you were talking about the recurring dream you were having with that big nice, cold … what did you say the glass was doing? Sweating? Sweating big beads of sweat and after you drank it you woke up sweating. I'm no therapist but I think you should go to AA. Eh … I started drinking when I was thirteen and I've been drinking every day since. It was over Christmas and sure you just woke up and had a beer for breakfast and I just kept it going. Rolled it over, all these years. No one cared. No one cared about whatever happened to me about *(to themselves)* what Jim fixed for me. I don't care either to be honest. Probably going to go to the pub after this coz I need a drink. If it was so bad for us it wouldn't be legal, would it? *(Beat.)*

When does the pain stop? Isn't that why you're all here? It makes the pain stop? No? Right. Pub?

SCREAMING

CHARACTER and their companions are holed up try-ing to survive in a world where demons roam the night.

CHARACTER. It always starts with the screaming. In the pitch black. When the sun has long since left us for the night. Not exactly a scream, not quite a howl but something in between. When I first heard it, my first instinct was to find it and kill it. I guess it's because something that makes a sound like that ... shouldn't exist. I had an urge to grab any weapon I could and follow the screams and kill it. I think that's what it wanted. The screams became ... monotonous after a while, it was bizarre, we were cowering in that room for hours. It screamed outside like it had something stuck in its throat. Like a gurgle. Like it forgot how to scream properly, like it couldn't stick to the script any-more. Charlie started us laughing. That camarad-erie in the midst of death. Only he could do that. Charlie ran to it, we followed, weapons in hand, until we saw it. Now we're back here, Charlie's the one screaming and nobody's laughing anymore.

SO, I GOT A DOG

CHARACTER lives in a world of their own making ... and still suffers.

CHARACTER. Good boy. Good boy. He bit someone today. For the first time. So good. They haven't let me get any sleep for the last two weeks. Cutting grass, playing football, banging on the door asking for the ball back but then when I give it back to them it just comes over the wall again, five minutes later. What's the point? They just do it to piss me off. So, I got a dog. Now they're too scared to kick the ball over. He's a beauty. Aren't you boy? Who's a good boy? I just want to sleep to stop the voices in my head. When I got out of bed this afternoon there was a delivery, but I didn't order anything, I never order anything that's how they find you. He barked and he barked ... like this ... *(The Character barks.)* If you answer the door, they know where you live and as I was telling this to the delivery man ... she bit him! They will think twice before coming to my house, no? I think he was looking for number twenty but I am twenty-two. No matter, huh? Good, girl. Good, girl. Hold on. There's someone at the door. *(The character growls.)*

SUP?

The character deals drugs and hangs outside the shop answering calls on their phone. The phone rings, they answer.

CHARACTER. Sup? Yeah? No. So? And? And? Fuck off. No. Maybe so. Yeah, yeah, yeah. Are your fuckin' hormones at you again? So? Fuck it did she hear? Sorry. I said fuckin' sorry. Don't put her on. *(Beat.)* Hello?

Yeah. Didn't do nuthin'. So? She's annoyin' me. *(Beat.)* Right. Right. Right. I'm workin'. Yeah, I'm working. Fuck's sake like. Yeah. Yeah. Five fifty bags. Yeah. Alright. Yeah. *(Beat.)* Dunno. Chips. Grand. Grand, I said grand. Yeah. Right. Right see ye. Yeah, yeah love you too. Here! Here! Don't bury them in gravy this time. Right. *(The character hangs up.)* Sap. *(They spit a big golly. The phone rings. They answer.)* Sup?

TAKING THE BINS OUT

The CHARACTER is approached by a former so-called friend.

CHARACTER. What are you doing here? Asking all about town for me and now this? Sneaking by the gaff when I'm putting the bins out? I told you I was done with you. Unless it's a big grovelling apology with you on your knees begging for forgiveness and a promise you'll leave here and join an Ashram in India for the rest of your life, I don't wanna hear it. Get out of my way. Friends? We're not friends? Parasite and host that's what we are. Guess which one you are...? Don't, don't you dare say host or I'll put you in the bin. You've no idea, do you? What friends do? Well here's what they don't do. They don't ridicule you because they're threatened by you. They don't impose themselves on you emotionally or ... physically. They don't ruin your good buzz with other good buzzers and try and drag you down into their cyclical hell. It means it's a cycle, you incompetent dickhead. A never-ending cycle with you at the centre. A black hole. Friends are for people with soul and you ain't got none. Now fuck off. I've to put the bins out.

TAXI'S HERE

Sam, an alcoholic, has been turning up at the CHAR-ACTER's house in progressively worse condition.

CHARACTER. Taxi's here. Hello? Your taxi is here. Get off my couch Sam. Off. This is the fourth cry for help I've gotten off you this month and you are well beyond the boy who called wolf at this stage. You're the boy who called … I dunno, just get off my couch. Up. I'm beyond helping you at this stage, I'm beyond it. No. I didn't say you were beyond help. That's what you think isn't it? You turn up at my house like this and you believe, in the very core of your being, that you're beyond help. All you want me to do is prove it to you. If I don't help you, in some shape or form, you'll have proved yourself right. You keep pushing and you keep pushing. You know I loved you. You know it nearly killed me sending you away but I'm not doing this to you. You are. *(Long beat.)* I'll cancel the taxi, but this the last time.

MY FAVOURITE JUMPER

The character confronts their partner, who is doing a clear out of old unused clothes.

CHARACTER. No! That's my favourite jumper! What are you doing? What? Gimme that. I'm not getting rid of it. No way. The sentimental value of this is … well it's priceless, that's what sentimental means. Look, dog hair. Or is it mine or yours. Of course it smells, it smells nice that's what it smells like. It smells of nice things, that's why I love it. *(The character sniffs different parts of the jumper.)* This part. Was when we were camping last month. I can still smell the wet logs that wouldn't catch. That was a nice memory. *(Sniffs again.)* Here. Here you can smell your perfume. See? I know it's faint but underneath everything else it's there. *(They turn it around and sniff.)* And here. Oh, God. I don't know what that is. That wasn't me. Okay. Well. Maybe wash it, but definitely don't throw it out. It just … it makes me feel warm when I wear it.

THE LEDGE

The Character attempts to talk a stranger down off a ledge.

CHARACTER. Hey! Hey! It's okay. It's alright. It's alright. I won't, I won't touch you don't worry. *(Beat.)* Probably a lot of worry got you here, huh? I'll just stand here for a bit, enjoy the view. It's a long way down, can you swim? *(Beat.)* Well then, it'll definitely do the job. You must have a lot of life inside you if you wanna do this. You're very brave. You are. It takes a lot of courage to get up to where you are now. You must have a tremendous amount of energy inside of you. A lot of pain? Pain is energy, my friend. It takes an almost unbelievable amount of energy to take a life. You've got the courage and the energy to be here, you've the courage and the energy to end it all, but most of all, you've the courage and the energy to get through the pain. You do have energy, the power you have inside you. It feels like gravity itself is crushing you down, right? Your head feels dark, like the walls are closing in, you've gone beyond feeling anything? That's a tremendous amount of energy. Think of what you could do with that if you just turned around.

YOU, YEAH. YOU.

The CHARACTER berates themselves in front of a mirror.

CHARACTER. You, yeah you. I'm talking to you. You ugly worthless wretch. Everyone hates you, you know that. Everyone wants you dead. They do. Of course, they do you're the worst thing in the world. Nobody likes you, they think you're a joke. A fool. An idiot. *(A pause as the character reflects on the weight of the words.)* Why do I think like this? Do I really think like this? Does anyone else? Of course they don't, you can see that for yourself every day on your shitty phone. God you're so stupid. *(A pause. A moment of justified anger.)* No. you listen here. You are a good, kind, decent person. You stop it now, you stop talking to yourself like that. Stop. You are loveable. You're not gonna boss me around anymore. I'm gonna go out there and show them. *(An abrupt pause. Maybe a laugh.)*

Who am I even talking to? Who am I talking to?

ACKNOWLEDGE-
MENT

I am, and will forever be, eternally grateful for the support, collaboration and encouragement from the following.

All the Actors who graciously gave their effort, skill and enthusiasm for all the characters in the Purgatory; archaic seasons so far (Including the ones not published in this collection). I really cannot thank you enough.

Niamh Sweeney for her encouragement, belief and help in putting this collection into print. Ian and Luke of the collective productions who facilitated my playwrighting (and stage) debut. Ciara and John of Central Arts who helped me develop both in confidence and skill as a playwright. OC Productions for helping organize the Killarney showing of the plays and their support and encouragement. The late great, Brendan Grace for his inspiration and encouragement of my writing. John and everyone at the international Bar for their excellent venue and hospitality to the audience and crew. Johnnie and everyone at Bleecker Street Café & Bar for their continued support professionally and personally. The audiences for fulfilling their roles so generously and perfectly as the last remaining piece of the theatre artform.

Most recently, a big thank you to author and entertainer Sean Kelly for his belief and collaboration, Daithi Harrison for the same.

And lastly, Nora the dog, without whom this book would have been finished sooner. I hope to see you all back on stage sooner rather than later.

Luke Corcoran, Summer 2021